'When you s...... a deadly killer gas, what sort of gas?' asked Jack.

'A gas that disintegrates people's bones,' replied Dorothy. 'In fact, it's so powerful that just one whiff of the gas and people's bones fall apart and they turn into human jellyfish.'

'Urgh!!' said Kate and Michael together in disgust.

Jack stared at Dorothy, stunned as the full horror of the situation hit him.

'But my friend Cynthia's making that formula up right at this very moment. If she breathes it, she'll die!'

UNCLE JACK
AND
OPERATION GREEN

by Jim Eldridge

Illustrated by
Ann Johns

RED FOX

A Red Fox Book
Published by Arrow Books Limited
20 Vauxhall Bridge Road, London SW1V 2SA

An imprint of the Random Century Group
London, Melbourne, Sydney, Auckland
Johannesburg and agencies throughout the world

Red Fox edition 1990

Set in Times
by Deltatype Ltd, Ellesmere Port

Made and printed in Great Britain by
Courier International Ltd, Tiptree, Essex

ISBN 0 09 979140 4

With thanks to Jeremy Swan, without whom there would have been no BBC TV series, and without which there would have been no book.

Contents

CHAPTER ONE

How It All Started

It all started because of Uncle Jack, although in the part of West London where he lived, this was not unusual as so many things seemed to start because of Uncle Jack. Barely a week would pass without the *West London Gazette* carrying a story that read: 'Jack Green, 40, a lecturer in Education at West London Polytechnic, was arrested today, charged with walking down Acton High Street dressed as a duck in a manner calculated to disturb the peace'; or 'Local environmentalist and green campaigner, Jack Green, said this week . . .' and then would follow some statement by Uncle Jack concerning the careless dumping of toxic waste, the irresponsible transportation of radioactive materials; or there would be a photograph of Uncle Jack standing in front of a tree, trying to prevent it being cut down.

As a result, local opinion about Uncle Jack was divided. There were those like his niece, Kate Stevens, and her teacher at Winfield Middle School, Miss Arabella Taylor, who thought that Uncle Jack was a hero of the age, prepared to put himself in the front line in his efforts to save the planet from destruction. On the other hand his nephew, Michael (Kate's brother), and Jack's sister, as well as many local Council officials thought that Jack was a pain in the bottom. In fact, in Michael's opinion, Jack was an embarrassment to the family. As he often said to

Kate – 'Do you realize everyone knows that the lunatic who chained himself to the railings outside the Water Company last week is our uncle? They must think we're potty, too!'

Certain local business people also didn't like Uncle Jack's activities, mainly because they interfered with the big profits they made from things like pouring battery acid down drains (where it eventually got back into the water supply) or treating food with radiation (so that it looked shinier and lasted longer in the shops), destroying all the goodness in it. (Jack always said of irradiated food: 'Of course it looks shinier, it's radioactive! It's a wonder it doesn't glow in the dark!')

Anyway, the particular series of chaotic events which became known by MI5 as 'Operation Green' started when Jack went to speak at Kate and Michael's school about the destruction of the South American rain forests. Miss Taylor, of course, was in attendance, lapping up every word as Jack showed slides of the rain forests of Brazil and told the children how their destruction threatened not only the natives and the wild life of South America, but also the world's weather.

'We've got one planet,' he said, 'and it's like an apple. If one bit of it goes rotten, after a while that rottenness spreads to the rest, and we end up trying to live on a rotten apple.'

After the talk, Miss Taylor was the first to grab Uncle Jack and congratulate him.

'Uplifting!' she enthused. 'So much knowledge, such wonderful concern!'

'Well, thank you,' smiled Uncle Jack, a bit taken aback by Miss Taylor's enthusiasm.

Miss Taylor turned to Kate and Michael.

'Well, Michael,' she said, 'aren't you going to congratulate your uncle on his performance?'

'I have never seen this man before in my life,' said Michael defensively, peeved that schools should spend their time inviting in eccentric uncles to show people up.

Jack grinned. 'Poor Michael,' he said. 'I think sometimes I embarrass him.'

'Nonsense!' said Miss Taylor. 'The world needs to be embarrassed.'

Michael made noises at the back of his throat which suggested that he didn't entirely agree with this point of view. However, Miss Taylor was now ignoring Michael and concentrating on Jack with zealous vigour.

'And what is your next campaign going to be, Mr Green?' she demanded.

'Water pollution,' replied Jack, 'though right now I'm off to the local office of Gaschem Chemicals to complain about the smoke from their chimneys. It's absolutely disgusting. As well as covering all the surrounding houses with dust, who knows what sort of elements the smoke contains?'

The thought of Jack taking on the local giants of the chemical industry obviously filled Miss Taylor with a sense of excitement.

'Wonderful!' she trilled rhapsodically. 'And are you going to chain yourself up? Tie yourself to their chimneys?'

'Er . . . not exactly,' said Jack, again slightly taken aback by her enthusiasm. 'I'm going to deliver a letter expressing my concern.'

Miss Taylor's face fell. She obviously expected

something a bit more daring from Uncle Jack than just writing a letter, something a bit more like Indiana Jones or James Bond. After all, this was Jack Green, the man who had delivered a dustbinful of toxic waste to the Council Health Department to publicise the way they dumped waste without taking proper safety precautions. This was the man who had walked down the High Street dressed up as a duck to highlight the problems suffered by wildlife in the area. A letter? It was a bit of a let-down.

Jack saw Miss Taylor's face drop and gave her a reassuring smile.

'Don't worry,' he said. 'If they don't do anything about the pollution, perhaps then I'll chain myself to their front door.'

'Oh, good!' said Miss Taylor, enthusiastically. Then an idea struck her. 'I'll tell you what I'll do!' she said. 'I'll write a letter of protest as well, and you can deliver it along with yours, on my behalf!' And, to the shock of Kate and Michael, she nestled closer to Jack. 'We'll be "green" partners,' she murmured conspiratorially.

Not if I have anything to do with it, thought Jack, edging away slightly. However, he said aloud: 'I'd love to deliver your letter for you,' and with that Miss Taylor went off to find some headed notepaper to write on.

'Can I come with you, Uncle Jack?' piped up Kate suddenly.

'I don't think that's a good idea,' replied Uncle Jack. 'You know what your mother thinks of my activities.'

'But I want to save the planet, too,' said Kate. 'After all, I live on it as well.'

This was an argument that Jack couldn't defeat.

'And it's not as if you're going to chain yourself up, are you?' persisted Kate. 'You said so just now to Miss Taylor.'

'Or dress up as a parrot?' added Michael, not wanting to be involved in any mad scheme of his uncle's, but feeling that unless he threw in his two-pennyworth people would forget he was around.

'I *was* dressed up as a duck,' corrected Jack.

'You *looked* like a parrot,' said Michael.

'You're only going to deliver a letter,' finished Kate.

Jack sighed. He knew when he was beaten.

'Okay,' he said. 'But we just deliver the letters, and then we go straight back home. Michael, you'd better tell your mum where we've gone so she won't worry.'

'Huh,' scowled Michael, 'I always get the rotten jobs.'

At that point Miss Taylor reappeared with a brown envelope, which she gave to Jack.

'There!' she said proudly. 'My letter. I've told them they must stop their filthy smoke from contaminating this planet! That should put them in their place!'

So it was that Uncle Jack and Kate set off after school towards Gaschem Chemicals with two letters of protest – his and the one from Miss Taylor. In fact, on reflection, it was Miss Taylor's letter that caused all the trouble, so perhaps in this case it might be true to say that everything really began because of Miss Taylor.

* * *

When Jack and Kate arrived with the letters at the plush offices of Gaschem Chemicals, the reception desk was empty. It just so happened that the receptionist had chosen that very moment (it being a slack sort of day) to go to the coffee machine and get herself a cup of coffee.

Kate and Jack stood like two lost souls in the empty reception area.

'What do we do?' asked Kate.

'There's only one thing we can do,' said Jack. 'I'll simply leave my letter here on the desk and the receptionist will find it when she comes back.'

And with that Jack and Kate left, only half aware of the closed circuit security TV camera in the ceiling that was recording all that happened at five-second intervals. Jack and Kate had barely left the building when Kate remembered something.

'You forgot to leave Miss Taylor's letter!' she said.

'Good lord!' said Jack. 'So I did!' And he took Miss Taylor's letter from his inside pocket. 'I'll take it straight back in now.'

Jack was just turning to go back into Gaschem Chemicals, when the glass doors of the building opened and a man dressed in cleaner's overalls and carrying a brown envelope rushed out and bashed straight into Jack with a thump! as their heads collided.

There was one of those moments of confusion as the two men staggered around on the pavement, each holding his head and saying things like 'Ouch!' and 'Ooo!', before they realized that they had both dropped their brown envelopes on the pavement. Jack reached down for the brown envelope that he thought was the one containing Miss Taylor's letter,

but before he could reach it the man leapt upon it, snatched it up, and ran off at a speed that would have done credit to an Olympic sprinter. Jack rubbed his head where he had bumped it and picked up the remaining brown envelope from the pavement.

'Funny bloke,' he said. 'Oh well, let's deliver Miss Taylor's letter.'

It was only when Jack and Kate were once more in Gaschem's still empty reception area that Jack realized there was something different about the brown envelope he was holding. It didn't appear the same as the one Miss Taylor had given him. In fact, it felt somehow *different*. Jack checked the flap of the envelope. It was unsealed. Puzzled, Jack opened the envelope and took out the piece of paper that was inside. He looked at it, and then announced to Kate:

'This isn't Miss Taylor's letter!'

'What?' said Kate.

'That man picked up the wrong envelope!'

And with that, Jack rushed out of the building, intent on catching up with the man in the cleaner's overalls. Kate followed her uncle, but by the time they got out of the building it was too late – the man was long gone.

'Missed him!' said Jack ruefully.

'I wonder if what he dropped is important?' asked Kate, looking over her uncle's shoulder at the piece of paper.

'I haven't the faintest idea what it is,' admitted Jack. 'It's all loads of numbers and letters.'

They studied it together. It seemed to consist of lots of things marked 'X' and 'Ze' equalling something else called BF49 and all multiplied by lots of different numbers with decimal points in them.

17

'Perhaps it's his pools coupon?' suggested Kate.

'Whatever it is, we've got to get it back to him,' said Jack. Then an idea struck him. 'I know! I'll put an ad in the Gazette saying "Will the man who picked up the wrong envelope outside Gaschem Chemicals on Thursday please contact Jack Green at Flat 3 etcetera etcetera." '

'That's brilliant!' said Kate. Then she frowned, thoughtfully. 'But say he doesn't read the local paper?'

Jack thought about it, and then shrugged.

'All I can do is try,' he said. 'Anyway, it can't be that important or he wouldn't have been carrying it around so carelessly.'

And with that Jack and Kate went, with neither of them the tiniest bit aware of just how very, very, very wrong Jack was about the importance of that piece of paper.

CHAPTER TWO

The Death Gas

The managing director and the chairman of
Gaschem were playing Snakes and Ladders in the
chairman's office, under the pretence that it was a
'scientific experiment', when the door burst open
and their chief scientist, Simon Simpkins, burst in
with the terrible news.

'It's gone!' he screamed. 'It's gone! We're
doomed! It's gone!'

The chairman and the managing director looked
at him, annoyed at this interruption. The managing
director was particularly annoyed as he had just
been about to go up a ladder, and now his move
would quite likely be made invalid by this sudden
intrusion.

'For heaven's sake, Simpkins!' he snorted. 'Get
hold of yourself! What's gone?'

'The formula for the secret gas we're working on!
It's been stolen!'

'Surely not,' said the chairman. 'Couldn't it have
fallen on the floor, or into a wastebasket, or
something?'

'No,' said Simpkins, 'because I know who stole it!'

Simpkins produced a video cassette. He put it into
the video machine on the chairman's desk and
switched it on.

'This is the video from the closed circuit TV
camera in Reception. Watch.'

19

The men watched, and as they did they saw on the monitor the doors of the reception open and Jack and Kate enter the building. The next picture was of a few seconds later and showed Jack leaning over the reception desk. Then, a few seconds later still, there was Jack opening a brown envelope and taking out a piece of paper. The next shot was a close-up of the piece of paper in Jack's hands.

'There!' squeaked Simpkins. 'The formula!'

'Good grief!' groaned the managing director.

The last shot showed Jack and Kate leaving the building, Jack with the piece of paper still in his hand.

'Good Lord!' moaned the managing director, even louder this time.

The chairman frowned.

'I know that man from somewhere,' he said thoughtfully.

'We all do,' said the managing director. 'It's that terrible "green" man.'

'Green?' said the chairman. 'He looked an ordinary sort of colour to me, though I suppose you can't see it so well on the video . . .'

'Not "green" as in colour,' snapped the managing director. ' "Green" as in name. He's always on the TV or in the papers complaining about things. I saw him on the news earlier today, chained to some railings for some cause or other.'

'Oh, yes!' said the chairman, relieved now he knew what everyone was talking about. 'I recognize him now! He was in the High Street a couple of weeks ago, dressed up as a duck.'

'What on earth was he doing dressed up as a duck?' asked the managing director, in astonishment.

20

'Who knows?' said the chairman. 'Perhaps his suit was at the cleaners'.'

'The point is,' snapped Simpkins, determined not to let his two bosses forget the reason for his having come in, 'he's got our formula!'

'But what on earth would he want with our formula?' asked the chairman.

'To embarrass us, of course!' raged Simpkins. It's the sort of thing he does, showing up companies that "pollute the environment", as he calls it. And this new gas of ours is just the sort of thing he's totally against.'

'But how would he even know about it?' asked the chairman. 'I thought it was supposed to be a secret.'

'How do these people find these things out,' mused the managing director, bitterly.

'How he found it out is neither here nor there,' said Simpkins. 'The thing is, what are we going to do?'

'Simple,' said the chairman. 'Call the police and have him arrested.'

Both Simpkins and the managing director threw up their hands in horror at the suggestion.

'No, no!' said the managing director. 'That's the last thing we should do!'

'Right,' agreed Simpkins emphatically. 'This gas is supposed to be a secret weapon for the Government. It won't be much of a secret if we tell the Police about it.'

'Exactly,' said the managing director.'

'So what *do* we do?' asked the chairman, feeling more and more helpless with every passing second.

'There's only one thing we can do,' replied the managing director. 'We call in MI5.'

22

M, head of MI5, paced around his office. On the wall behind him were blow-ups of three still photographs taken from the Gaschem security video, showing Jack both with and without the secret formula, and one of him with Kate. M tapped the nearest photograph with a pointer and turned to Dorothy Greckle.

'This is the man, Agent 7,' said M. 'Jack Green.'

Dorothy peered forward to examine the photographs closer. Then she sat back with a smile on her face.

'He looks like a kind man,' she said cheerfully.

M glared at Dorothy.

'He is a villain of the worst sort, Agent 7,' he corrected her. 'That formula he is holding in his hand could bring this Government – nay, this country – to its knees!'

Oh dear, thought Dorothy, I've dropped a brick again.

M looked furtively about him, as if to make sure there were no spies within hearing distance, and then said in low tones:

'What I am about to say is in the strictest confidence. No one outside these four walls must ever know about it.'

Dorothy leaned forward and lowered her voice to a suitably secret level.

'Absolutely, sir,' she whispered. 'You can count on me.'

'Right,' said M. 'This formula is for a secret gas which disintegrates bones while leaving the rest of the body untouched. One whiff of this gas and the whole human being just collapses internally and turns into a human jellyfish.'

'Ugh!' said Dorothy, quite revolted. 'How awful!'

'But necessary, Agent 7,' said M.

Actually what would have been even more awful, at least for M, is if he'd known that at that very moment his oh-so-secret conversation with Agent 7 was being listened to at both the American and the Russian embassies. Their spies had planted secret microphones in M's office: the Americans' in the bowl of flowers on M's desk, and the Russians' underneath his telephone.

In their own separate offices, each unaware that the other was also eavesdropping, the CIA boss, Herman Shoemaker, and the boss of the NFRSS (formerly called CHEKA, also formerly called OGPU, also formerly NKVD; MVD/MGB, and KGB, and now called the Newly Formed Russian Secret Service), Mikhael Rinzikov, listened agog as they heard M unfold to Dorothy the story of the secret gas.

'Our fear,' continued M, 'is that he may leak the existence of this formula to the Press.'

'But do you really think this man would do an underhand thing like that?' asked Dorothy.

'And why shouldn't I think it?' demanded M.

'Well . . . ' said Dorothy, and she looked at the photographs again. 'He's got honest eyes.'

'Honest eyes!' snorted M. 'Let me tell you, Agent 7, this man is capable of anything. Why, only last week he walked up and down his local high street dressed as a duck!'

'Good heavens!' said Dorothy, looking at the photos of Jack with eyes anew.

'Your job,' continued M, 'is to get to know this man. Find out what he's up to. Get under his skin. Get hold of the formula, and then . . .' And here M's voice dropped an octave lower with menace . . . 'Then we'll deal with him.'

'Yes, sir,' said Dorothy, a little uncertainly. She didn't like the sound of this 'dealing with him', she'd never been too keen on people being hurt. Especially when they looked as honest and law-abiding as this Jack Green seemed to. Then another thought struck her. 'But what about the little girl?'

'Little girl?' frowned M. 'What little girl?'

Dorothy pointed to Kate in the photograph. 'That one,' she said. 'Surely he wouldn't have done anything like stealing a secret formula when he had that little girl with him. It would have put her at risk.'

M shook his head, the thought crossing his mind once again whether Dorothy Greckle was really the right kind of person to be a secret agent.

'A man who is capable of dressing up as a duck is capable of anything, Agent 7,' he said. 'I imagine the girl's a decoy.'

'A decoy duck, eh, sir!' joked Dorothy.

M gave her a glare which showed he was not amused.

'Sorry, sir,' said Dorothy. 'It was just a humorous thought that occurred to me.'

'Was it?' said M. 'Well, for the moment you'd better stop thinking humorous thoughts and make a note of this man Green's address. And remember, this information is Absolutely Top Secret. His name is Jack Green and he lives at Flat 3, 26 Ashburnham Gardens.'

And that was how the CIA and the NFRSS got hold of Jack's address.

CHAPTER THREE

Jose Cuervo

Meanwhile, what about Jose Cuervo? (Who, you may ask, is Jose Cuervo? Or, to give him his full title, Generalissimo San Carlos Perdita San Maria Jose Cuervo, leader of the Revolutionary Army of the New Right from the tiny Central American country of San Perdino, and the man in the cleaner's overalls who had bumped into Jack outside the offices of Gaschem and had dropped the envelope containing the formula for the deadly gas.)

For some six years now Generalissimo Jose Cuervo had been trying to overthrow the government of his country, a government which he insisted was totally Communist and ought to be shot *en masse*. The problem that Jose Cuervo had was that most of the people of his country didn't agree with him. The government was actually a perfectly ordinary, placid, democratically elected government that went about the business of governing in the way that most governments do – which was to ignore the people completely and just hold meetings and talk all day. The people were quite happy for the government to do this, because while the government kept talking no one was getting shot and the people could get on with the business of living.

For Jose Cuervo this was not good enough. He wanted San Perdino to be a forceful country, with himself as El Presidente Generalissimo San Carlos

Perdita San Maria Jose Cuervo – president for life. He had tried to get elected as such, but had only gained seven votes. After the election he had scoured the country to find the other six people who had voted for him, and along with these had formed his Revolutionary Army with which he intended to overthrow the government of San Perdino and have himself appointed Dictator. The main problem that he faced was that a Revolutionary Army with only five people in it couldn't achieve much, especially as five of the six were high-ranking officers, who didn't like being told what to do. There was himself as Generalissimo, two captains and three lieutenants, which left only one private soldier in the ranks, who was getting fed up with being bossed around by the other five and kept threatening to leave.

To solve this problem Jose Cuervo had looked abroad. What his army needed, he reasoned, was a Dangerous Weapon which he could use to win his revolution. It was this search for such a Dangerous Weapon that had brought him to Britain, and finally to the offices of Gaschem, where he had heard that just such a weapon was being developed on behalf of the British Government (for peaceful purposes only, he was assured) – a gas that disintegrated the bones of people but left buildings and property intact.

To get hold of the formula had been simple: he had taken a job at Gaschem as a cleaner and then spent weeks finding out where the formula for the deadly gas was kept. Then, today, he had struck! It had been the work of seconds to slip into the laboratory, snatch the formula, and then get out of the building as fast as he could – a plan that had worked perfectly. Well, almost perfectly. (He still had a bump on his head from that idiot man he had crashed into as he was leaving the building.) But that was of no consequence; what was important was that he was back, safe and sound in his little bed-sitter with the formula safely in his hands!

Cuervo took the brown envelope from his pocket and kissed it.

'Now, at last!' he crowed. 'Those fools in San Perdino will laugh on the other side of their faces now that I have . . . this!'

Triumphantly, he opened the envelope and took out . . . Miss Taylor's letter.

Cuervo's face went a sort of pasty, yellowy white and his mouth dropped open.

'Heuvos a la flamenca!' he said, shocked (which is Spanish for 'I'll have an omelette!' and means, in this case, 'Oh dear, oh dear, what has happened here?'). Then realisation dawned. 'That-a man who bump into me, *he* must have-a picked up the formula!'

Cuervo knew that he had to get that formula back at all costs! Frantically, he scanned the letter he had in his hands for clues as to the identity of the man who had taken it, but of clues there were very few. All there was on the paper was Miss Taylor's few brief words to Gaschem, urging them to 'stop your filthy smoke!', and her signature: 'Miss Arabella Taylor'.

'This Miss Arabella Taylor!' mused Cuervo. 'She must know this man.'

Cuervo again examined the letter, especially the letterhead.

'Winfield Middle School. Okay! Tomorrow I go to this Winfield Middle School and get this Miss Taylor to tell me who this man is and where I can find him!'

Meanwhile, what about Uncle Jack? In his own way he was also suffering, but in a way that he had suffered many times before.

When Jack returned Kate back home they were met by Jack's not altogether happy sister, Kate's mum, Elizabeth.

'What have you been up to with my daughter?' she demanded as she opened the door to them.

'Nothing,' protested Jack. 'We just went to deliver a letter to Gaschem to protest about the pollution from their chimneys.'

'Exactly!' said Elizabeth, grim-faced. 'You're getting her involved in your lunatic activities. I've told you before, I don't want you involving Kate and Michael.'

'We are involved, Mum,' said Kate. 'It's our future we're talking about.'

'Hush,' said Elizabeth. 'You shouldn't listen to your uncle.'

By now they were in the living room, where Michael was reading a comic and Kate's dad, Edward Stevens, was busy working on yet another of his matchstick models.

It was Edward's ambition to construct a model of the Taj Mahal completely out of matchsticks. So far the only model he had completed successfully was of a small lighthouse without windows, but he was building up to the Taj Mahal in steady stages. He was now working on a model of Big Ben which was slowly, ever ever so slowly, ascending match by match towards the clock face. He hoped that the same wouldn't happen to this one as had happened to most of his previous models: namely, they had got so far and then had collapsed at the crucial moment, usually just before the roof went on.

Edward viewed Jack's arrival with nervousness. Whenever his brother-in-law came round it usually led to an argument between Jack and Elizabeth, which meant that his frail matchstick models were at risk. It is not a good idea, Edward reflected, to build something as fragile as a model out of matchsticks with two members of the Green family in hot debate, especially when they threw things like cushions at each other. (Although Edward had to admit, without, he hoped, being disloyal, that it was Elizabeth who did most of the throwing. Jack, as an advocate of non-violence, restricted himself to words. The trouble was, it was Jack's words that usually led Elizabeth to throw something.)

'I can't see what you can object to about my views,' said Jack. 'What I'm trying to do is to make this planet a safer place for future generations, and that includes your own children.'

'I don't disagree with your views,' said Elizabeth. 'What I object to is the way you go about them. Things like chaining yourself to drilling rigs to stop people drilling.'

'What's wrong with that?' asked Jack. 'It worked. It got our campaign on the television news and it stopped them drilling for that nuclear waste dump.'

'Exactly!' said Elizabeth. 'It put you on television, chained up!'

'That was the point of it,' said Jack. 'To bring home to people what is happening. To show people the *truth*.'

'That may be what you intended,' said Elizabeth, 'but what happens is that people get to see Edward's brother-in-law on the TV depicted as a criminal!'

'I am not a criminal!' protested Jack.

'You were arrested,' pointed out Elizabeth.

'Yes, but that doesn't make me a criminal,' said Jack. 'Anyhow, what's all this got to do with Edward? I didn't involve him.'

'Edward can't help being involved because he is your brother-in-law,' said Elizabeth. 'And you seem to forget that Edward has his position as Assistant Manager at the bank to think of. It reflects on Edward whenever you do something outrageous like dressing up as a duck, or hanging a banner from a bridge . . .'

'Or chaining yourself to railings,' added Michael, just to let people know he was still there.

'Quiet,' said Elizabeth. 'You shouldn't be listening.'

'Personally, I think you're making a huge fuss over nothing,' said Jack. 'Especially in this case. After all, all I've done is deliver a letter. What "outrageous" things could possibly arise as a result of that?'

Kate and Michael were about to find out.

CHAPTER FOUR

Kidnapped!

At five to nine the next morning, Kate and Michael were walking along the corridor of Winfield Middle School on their way to their respective classrooms, discussing the idiocy of adults in general, and their closest relatives in particular.

'What gets me,' complained Michael, 'is the fact that we're supposed to keep quiet and not even listen. As far as they're concerned we might as well not exist but just be kept in cupboards and brought out for Christmas and holidays.'

'Uncle Jack isn't like that,' defended Kate. 'Uncle Jack listens to us.'

'Uncle Jack is an embarrassment,' said Michael.

Kate was about to defend her favourite uncle against this charge, when she suddenly realized that she had a picture in her bag that she was supposed to give to Miss Wilkins.

'Hang on,' she told Michael, 'I won't be a second.'

Michael looked for a convenient place to lean while he waited for his sister to carry out her errand. He was just wondering whether to lean against the door of the stock room or against a radiator, when a strange-looking man suddenly appeared beside him. The reason that he appeared strange to Michael was because, from the ankles upwards, he was dressed as the archetypal City businessman, complete with bowler hat and umbrella, but on his feet he wore sandals.

'Excuse-a me,' the man said. 'Can-a you tell me where I find-a Miss . . .' and here Cuervo (for it was he) took out Miss Taylor's letter and checked the name, '. . . Miss Arabella Taylor.'

'Yes,' said Michael, always keen to help. 'Her classroom's along this corridor and round the corner. Room 7.'

'Thank-a you,' smiled Cuervo politely, and then went off in search of Room 7.

Michael was just watching him disappear round the corner when Kate reappeared.

'Done,' she said. 'Who was that I heard you talking to?'

'Some man,' said Michael. 'He wanted to know where Miss Taylor's room was.'

'Oh?' said Kate, interested. 'What did he look like?'

Michael snorted.

'He looked like an idiot!' he said.

Miss Taylor certainly thought Cuervo seemed out of place when she heard a knock on her classroom door and turned to behold the apparition of the perfect City gent (except for the sandals).

'Yes?' she said.

'Excuse-a me,' smiled Cuervo, 'are you Miss Arabella Taylor?'

'I am indeed,' replied Miss Taylor. 'What can I do for you?'

By way of answer, Cuervo produced her letter to Gaschem and presented it to her.

'I hope you can help me. I find-a this letter you write . . .'

Miss Taylor took the letter and smiled, pleased.

'Oh yes, I gave this to Mr Green yesterday . . .'

She stopped as an awful thought crossed her mind, then demanded suspiciously: 'Are you from Gaschem?'

'Er . . . no,' said Cuervo.

At that, Miss Taylor brandished the letter at Cuervo and demanded accusingly: 'Then how did you get hold of this letter which I gave to Mr Green?'

Cuervo was stumped. What should he do? Telling the truth was out of the question – Cuervo hadn't told the truth since he was seven years old and he was a bit out of practice. He could make up some story, but that might only lead to Miss Taylor asking more questions. He could also hear the sounds of children approaching down the corridor towards the classroom. He made up his mind; this was no time for niceties. Miss Taylor gave a little scream as Cuervo suddenly grabbed her by the arm in a tight grip.

'Lissen!' he snarled menacingly. 'I don't-a have time! Where is this Mr Green?'

Miss Taylor glared back at him, defiantly.

'I don't know who you are,' she said, 'but I don't like your attitude. Get out of my classroom this instant!'

'Lissen . . .!' snarled Cuervo again, but at that moment Kate and Michael appeared in the doorway and saw what looked like Miss Taylor in the romantic grip of the odd-looking stranger.

'Oh, excuse us, Miss Taylor,' said Kate, blushing. Then she recognized Cuervo.

'It's the man who dropped the envelope,' she said to Michael.

'And you are the little girl!' yelled Cuervo, recognizing Kate. And with that, Cuervo released Miss Taylor and pounced towards Kate, intent on grabbing her. He was going to use her as a hostage to force Jack into giving him back the formula.

Kate and Michael had no idea of the plan in Cuervo's mind, but they knew that his designs on them were unhealthy from the way he pounced towards them with a menacing snarl on his face.

'Quick!' said Michael. 'Run!'

And then Michael and Kate were off down the corridor with Cuervo in hot pursuit close on their heels, dodging the children who were still coming into school.

Miss Taylor stood for a moment, recovering, and then she sprang into action. Whoever this man was, he was up to no good; and whatever he was up to no good about concerned Mr Green and Kate. He had to be stopped before he could get hold of the children!

'Headmaster . . .!' she called as she ran out of her classroom. 'Headmaster, help!'

Kate and Michael, meanwhile, had managed to throw Cuervo momentarily off their track amongst the mass of children in the corridors and had crept out to the safety of the school car park, where they were now hiding, crouched low between Miss Taylor's car and a battered old van.

'We'll stay here until the Police arrive,' said Michael.

'How do you know they'll arrive?' whispered Kate.

'You know what Miss Taylor's like,' said Michael. 'She's bound to call them.'

'But . . .' began Kate, and then stopped as Michael clapped his hand over her mouth.

'Sssssh!' whispered Michael.

Michael pointed, and Kate saw that Cuervo had just come out of the school and was now prowling around the car park, looking up and down the lines of teachers' cars.

'What shall we do?' quaked Kate. She wasn't enjoying this at all.

Neither, to be honest, was Michael. For once he'd rather be in school, having the most boring of lessons, than be hunted like this by this peculiar and sinister man. Then he had an idea.

'Keep watch,' he whispered to Kate.

Carefully, and doing his best to make no noise at all, Michael opened the rear door of the battered old van.

'We'll hide in here,' he whispered, 'until Miss Taylor or someone else arrives.'

Then, ever so quietly, Kate and Michael crept inside the back of the van and pulled the door noiselessly shut behind them.

Cuervo continued to prowl up and down the lines of cars. Those children must be here somewhere! He had seen them slip out of the school. Maybe they had left the school grounds altogether?

Just as he was thinking these thoughts, a shout behind him made him turn.

'There he is!'

Miss Taylor was just coming out of the school, closely followed by a rather nervous looking man, the headmaster, who wasn't completely sure that this chasing of dangerous people was really quite in his line.

No esta bien! swore Cuervo under his breath (which means 'This is not good') as Miss Taylor and the headmaster broke into a run towards him. That mad woman! groaned Cuervo. Did she not realize who she was dealing with? Very well, he would make a strategic retreat for the moment, but he, Generalissimo San Carlos Perdita San Maria Jose Cuervo, would return and find that little girl – his link with the mysterious Mr Green – later!

And with that Cuervo ran for the battered van in which Kate and Michael were hiding, jumped into the driver's seat, started the ignition and headed for the school gates and the main road.

CHAPTER FIVE

Operation Green

To say that Kate and Michael were shocked when the van started to move would be to understate the case. And when they peered up and realized that the driver was the very man they had been running away from, both their hearts nearly stopped! They cowered in the corner of the van, holding each other close with the same thought uppermost in both their minds . . . How do we get out of this?

Their escape lay in one of those coincidences that happen in life, like seeing someone who owes you money just when you find you haven't got enough for your bus fare. In this case Uncle Jack had decided that it was his duty to let Miss Taylor know that he had been unable to deliver her letter to Gaschem. So, finding that he had a spare hour because a lecture he was due to give that moring at the Polytechnic had been cancelled, he decided to go to the school and let Miss Taylor know exactly what had happened to her letter. It was just as Jack was going in through the school gates that Jose Cuervo drove out in the battered van, saw Jack in his mirror and stepped on the brake.

The van came to a halt with a loud Screechh!!, causing Jack to look round in case there had been an accident. Instead he saw Jose Cuervo jump down from the cab of the battered van. At the same time, the rear door of the van opened and Kate and Michael leapt out.

'Look out, Uncle!' called Michael. 'He's dangerous!'

'What . . . ? began Uncle Jack, bewildered by this sudden turn of events.

Jack turned back to face Cuervo to see just how dangerous this man was, when Cuervo spotted two uniformed policemen approaching, hurrying on their way to the school in answer to Miss Taylor's urgent 999 call.

'Caramba y bocadillo!' Cuervo yelled in fury. And with that, he jumped back into the van and raced off at great speed, nearly knocking the policemen down in the process.

'What in heaven's name is going on?' Jack demanded as Kate and Michael rushed up and clung to him. 'And how did you come to be in the back of that van?'

While Kate and Michael told their uncle what had happened, across the road and watching this scene was a young woman doing her best to look like someone out shopping. The fact that there were very few shops near the school did not deter her. Agent 7 of MI5, Dorothy Greckle, was doing her job of shadowing Jack Green, the object of surveillance in Operation Green – and nothing was going to stop her. She had followed Jack all the way from the Polytechnic and was now wondering what the incident she had just witnessed outside the school gates had all been about. Who had the man in the battered van been? Why had he driven off so furiously? Why had the two children been in the back of the van?

These same questions were also being asked independently by two men further along the same street, one disguised as a road sweeper and the other as a lamppost mender. The road sweeper was none other than CIA Agent Butch Brooks, and the lamppost mender was Georgio Nitzkov, Secret Agent for the NFRSS ('The Newly Formed Russian Secret Service,' he kept saying to himself, '*not* the KGB!')

Their task was also to watch Jack Green, and at the same time to keep an eye on MI5's agent and see what she could pick up. It had come to each man as more than a little annoying to find he was not alone in keeping surveillance on Jack Green and Dorothy Greckle.

Butch Brooks moved his broom a little nearer to the lamppost which Georgio was pretending to mend.

'What's the KGB doing here?' he hissed out of the corner of his mouth.

'I am not the KGB,' said Georgio defensively. 'I am from the NFRSS!'

'Okay,' said Butch. 'So what's the NFRSS's interest in this guy Jack Green?'

'Who?' demanded Georgio airily. 'Who is he?'

Curses! thought Butch. I've let the opposition know what we're on to! Drat and curses!

To try to throw Georgio off the scent, he said aloud: 'I haven't the faintest idea. It was just a name I made up.'

And with that he went back to sweeping the road.

* * *

The headmaster, meanwhile, had telephoned Kate and Michael's home to tell their mother what had happened. And so it was that Elizabeth Stevens joined her two children, Uncle Jack and Miss Taylor at the police station. The statements of Kate, Michael and Miss Taylor had all been taken down by a policewoman who was now suffering from writer's cramp after writing so much, especially because Miss Taylor had turned her version of events into something resembling a romantic novel. Elizabeth however, was not satisfied.

'The main thing,' she now told the sergeant who was in charge of the case, 'is to see that it doesn't happen again. I demand police protection for these children!'

'Wow!' said Kate, excited at the prospect. 'Does that mean we'll get bodyguards?'

This thought did not appeal to Michael.

'Huh!' he snorted. 'If that happens, we'll have the police watching our every move. No privacy!'

'It's for your own safety,' said Elizabeth.

'Very well,' said the sergeant resignedly. He knew when he was up against a formidable force, and Mrs Stevens was certainly that. 'If I can just have your full name, madam?'

Elizabeth hesitated.

'Actually,' she said, 'I'd rather you didn't use my name . . .'

'Oh?' said the sergeant.

'No,' said Elizabeth. 'You see, the children's father, Edward, has a very responsible position at the bank and I don't want his name linked with this kind of thing.'

The sergeant shook his head.

'I'm afraid we've got to have a name to put down, madam,' he said. 'After all, this is an official request that has to go through official channels. We can hardly have an "X" written all over official documents, can we?'

'What about using our name?' suggested Kate.

'Our name's the same as Mum and Dad's, banana brain,' pointed out Michael.

'You can use my name!' offered Miss Taylor, enthusiastically. 'It's Arabella Taylor. Arabella is spelt A . . . R . . .'

The sergeant regarded Miss Taylor sceptically. He was suspicious of people who volunteered information too readily; it usually meant they had something to hide.

'Are you related to these children . . . ? he asked in his best official manner.

'No, but . . .' began Miss Taylor.

The sergeant shook his head.

'For the purpose of these forms,' he said, 'it has to be a member of the family.'

'Very well,' said Elizabeth, and turned to Uncle Jack. 'We'll use your name. After all, *you* got them into this.' And to the sergeant she said: 'This is their uncle.'

The sergeant, content at last, flexed his writing fingers and poised his pen above the paper.

'And your name is, sir. . . ?' he asked.

'Jack Green,' said Uncle Jack, ever ready to help.

'I'm surprised you don't recognize him,' said Elizabeth acidly. 'You're always arresting him.'

The sergeant stopped writing and looked at Jack with eyes anew.

'You mean you're a known criminal . . . ?!' he demanded indignantly.

'No I am not!' said Jack with equal indignation.

'Yes you are,' said Mum. 'Chaining yourself to railings, hanging banners from bridges . . .'

Realization dawned on the sergeant, and his brow, previously darkening, now cleared. He stood up and positively beamed with friendliness and pleasure at Uncle Jack.

'*That* Jack Green!' he exclaimed. 'The Green Man! The environmental activist!'

'Yes . . .' admitted Jack with a modest smile.

'Well, well!' enthused the sergeant, still beaming broadly. 'I didn't recognize you in normal clothes. Usually when you come in here, you're covered in chains or dressed up as a duck . . . Please, allow me to shake your hand.'

And with that, the sergeant put out his hand and shook Jack's while Kate and Miss Taylor looked on with smiles of delight.

Elizabeth gaped incredulously at the sight.

'What on earth are you shaking his hand for?' she demanded of the sergeant. 'You normally arrest this man!'

The sergeant ignored her and gave Jack's hand another shake.

'A man dedicated to saving our planet for future generations,' he said approvingly. 'I've often said to my wife when we've seen you on the telly, protesting about something or other, "we need more people like him." ' Then he released Jack's hand. 'I'm sorry we have to keep arresting you, sir, but we do have our job to do.'

46

'I quite understand,' said Jack. 'No hard feelings at all.'

'Out of curiosity, Mr Green,' continued the sergeant, happy to have Jack in the station to chat to, 'What campaign are you currently involved in? Not that I want to arrest you for it,' he added hastily.

'My major campaign at the moment is to try to do something about the pollution of our local drinking water,' said Jack. 'I discovered a secret report last week that shows that the drinking water in this area contains levels of trichloroethylene at three times the World Health Organization guidelines.'

The sergeant nodded his head in agreement.

'You're telling me,' he said. 'The water in our house tastes dreadful! How's your campaign going?'

'I'm doing an interview about it on lunchtime TV tomorrow,' said Jack, 'so that'll be a major step forward for the campaign. I hope to pressurize the local water company to do something about it as a matter of urgency.'

'He's recording it at our school!' put in Miss Taylor, keenly. 'That's Winfield Middle School!'

'That's right,' nodded Jack. 'The producer thought that, as it affected the children . . .'

Jack didn't get a chance to explain the workings of the TV producer's mind, because Elizabeth had had just about enough of Jack stealing the limelight.

'I hate to interrupt this meeting of the Jack Green Appreciation Society,' she said through gritted teeth, 'But do you mind if we get on with the reason why we're here?'

'Certainly, madam,' said the sergeant. 'If you'll fill in the details of the children, address, and so on, I'll see that it gets into the proper channels.'

With that he passed Elizabeth an official-looking sheet of paper, while to Jack he passed an open autograph book.

'I know that this is unusual, but I wonder if I might have your autograph, Mr Green?' he asked.

'Why, of course,' said Jack, flattered, and he took the pen the sergeant offered.

'Just there,' pointed the sergeant. 'Under Chain-saw Hawkins.'

As Jack signed his autograph, Elizabeth finished filling in the official form and returned it to the sergeant. She did not look impressed. She was not sure how far to trust any police force that believed her idiot brother was someone to be proud of.

'There,' she said.

'Thank you madam,' said the sergeant. 'You can rest assured, the matter is now in the hands of the Police. You and the children can sleep safely in your beds.'

The sergeant watched the family troop out, and then wandered over to the computer, musing cheerfully to himself, 'Jack Green, eh? Well well!'

The sergeant sat down at the console and began to type in the information from the form Elizabeth had filled out. He had just typed in Uncle Jack's name and was half-way through typing his address, when he was startled by a humming and clicking from the computer. Then the monitor screen suddenly cleared, and on it appeared a message in capital letters that read: 'NO ACTION TO BE TAKEN ON JACK GREEN CASE. REPEAT, NO ACTION. IN HANDS OF SECRET SERVICE.'

The sergeant stared at the screen, taken aback.

'In the hands of the Secret Service, eh?' he said, impressed. 'Cor!'

Then a new message appeared on the screen: 'THIS MESSAGE WILL NOW SELF-DESTRUCT.' And with that, the screen went blank.

The sergeant shook his head in wonder at all these strange goings on. The Secret Service! Whatever next? He picked up the official form that Elizabeth had filled out, and all the statements that had been given by Kate, Michael and Miss Taylor, and dropped them into his wastepaper bin.

CHAPTER SIX

Spies

At the Stevens' house Edward had come home early from work in an attempt to get some more done on his matchstick model of Big Ben without interruption and, he hoped, without another argument between Elizabeth and Jack. So far, his model of Big Ben was still surviving, but only just. Elizabeth had actually picked up a cushion the day before to throw at Jack, but had decided against it at the last moment. As Edward glued another matchstick into position he heard the front door open, and then familiar voices, and he knew that his peace and tranquility was doomed once more. Within minutes the living room was once again full of his family: Kate, Michael, Elizabeth and Jack.

Kate and Michael did what they always did when they returned home: they switched on the television. However, they were only pretending to watch it: today their ears were all agog with yet another row (or 'debate' as Uncle Jack would call it) over the whole business of the mysterious man who had nearly driven off with Michael and Kate.

'Do you know what I think?' said Elizabeth, soon after the discussion had begun. 'I think this man knew that Edward holds a responsible position at the bank and was going to hold Kate and Michael hostage and make Edward hand over all the money.'

Jack shook his head.

'In that case, what was he doing with Miss Taylor?'

'I thought at first he was kissing her,' said Kate.

'Kissing Miss Taylor?!' said Michael, with much distaste at the thought. 'Yuk!'

'And you'll remember that Miss Taylor said he wanted to know where I lived,' said Uncle Jack. '*I* am the key to this.'

'You always have to be the centre of everything, don't you,' said Elizabeth, feeling put out. 'Well, Edward's important too, you know. Edward could be on television as well, if he wanted, and without chaining himself to things.''

A sudden thought struck Jack.

'Do you know what I think?' he said.

'No,' said Elizabeth, 'but I'm sure you're going to tell us.'

'I think he was after this piece of paper,' said Jack, and from his pocket he produced the sheet of paper the mystery man had dropped the day before.

'What are you talking about?' asked Elizabeth, puzzled.

'Yesterday, when I bumped into that man outside Gaschem, he was carrying this, and it looks to me like a formula for something.'

'Maybe he was a spy?' suggested Kate, excited by the idea.

'Exactly!' said Uncle Jack. 'An industrial spy, and I think he'd just stolen it.'

'What nonsense!' scoffed Elizabeth. 'Industrial spies?! Anything to make you feel important.'

'Well he didn't ask Miss Taylor where Edward lived, did he?' pointed out Jack, adding quickly, 'No offence, Edward,' because he was quite fond of his rather shy brother-in-law.

'And how do you propose to test this theory of yours?' asked Elizabeth.

'There is only one way,' said Jack.

He went to the phone, picked it up and began to dial.

'Who are you phoning?' asked Elizabeth.

Jack gave her a broad smile.

'Like a responsible citizen I'm phoning the chemical company and telling them . . .' At that point the switchboard at Gaschem answered, and Jack continued his conversation into the phone. 'Gaschem? Can I speak to the managing director, please . . . I see. Well, I'd like to leave a message for him. Tell him that Jack Green called and I think I've got something of yours . . . Ask him if he's missing any formula . . . That's right, I'll be over in about three quarters of an hour. Thank you.'

With that, Jack hung up and turned back to Elizabeth, Edward, Michael and Kate.

'You're going to look a complete idiot if it's not theirs,' pointed out Elizabeth.

'Who else could it belong to?' said Jack. He smiled to himself. 'You know, I can just picture that managing director's face when he gets my message that I'm bringing back his missing formula. I bet he'll welcome me with open arms!'

* * *

In that assumption, of course, Jack couldn't have been more wrong. The first reaction of the managing director and the chairman on receiving Jack's message was one of shock. As far as they were concerned, there could be only one reason why a known 'green' activist like Jack Green would be coming in to see them about this 'missing formula', which they knew perfectly well he had taken.

'He's coming in to gloat at us!' said the managing director. 'To let us know that *he* knows that *we* know that he's got the formula. I bet he wants to blackmail us in some way.'

'In what way?' asked the chairman, who wasn't as quick at grasping things as was the managing director.

The managing director spelt it out for him.

'For example,' he said, 'he might demand that unless we close down our factory, he'll expose us to the world as the people who invented this gas. Remember this is the most dreadful gas ever made. It disintegrates bones . . .'

'Please,' begged the chairman, feeling queasy. 'I've just had tea. What are we going to do?'

The managing director thought it over, and then came to a decision.

'We'll deny it,' he said.

'Deny what?' asked the chairman.

'That this formula is anything at all to do with us. We won't let him get the upper hand. We won't let him blackmail us!' He nodded vengefully. 'We'll also tell MI5 what he's up to. They'll soon sort him out!'

It was about half an hour later, as he was walking on his way to the offices of Gaschem, that Uncle Jack became aware of two men doggedly following him, one a short distance behind the other, one of the men cleaning the road with a broom as he walked, and the other stopping every now and then to tap a lamppost.

Good heavens! he thought, the Police have certainly acted fast in setting up this protection.

Then another thought struck him.

Hang on, they're not supposed to be watching *me*!

With that in mind he stopped in his tracks and went over to a bench to sit down. He didn't want to attract the attention of anyone who may have been watching the two men. After all, they were supposed to be undercover policemen.

As he expected, after a few minutes the man with the broom came up behind him and started sweeping the road about a metre away. Almost immediately, the other man arrived and started inspecting a nearby lamppost.

Jack gave a little cough, and then said, out of the corner of his mouth: 'Look, don't think I don't appreciate this, and it's not for me to tell you how to do your jobs. I know we asked the sergeant for protection, but it's *Kate* and *Michael* you're supposed to be watching. They're the ones who were nearly kidnapped.'

Butch and Georgio exchanged looks of astonishment and outrage. What was going on? How had this man spotted them?

Jack got up from the bench and then added, in a low voice, but with a smile to show that he wasn't being too critical: 'Also, I don't think it needs two of you to follow me. Think of the cost to the taxpayer. Anyway, best of luck, but do keep an eye on the kids.'

And with that Jack continued on his way to Gaschem.

At the offices of Gaschem the chairman and the managing director were getting more nervous by the minute as the time for Jack's arrival drew near. The chairman, in particular, seemed to be going to pieces.

'I don't think I can go through with this,' he said, wiping the sweat from his head with a piece of blotting paper.

'Of course you can,' said the managing director, firmly. 'Just remember, remain cool and calm. Relax. Don't panic. When he mentions the formula we laugh at him and pretend we don't know anything about it.'

'We laugh at him,' nodded the chairman gloomily, unconvinced. 'Right.' And he forced a laugh. 'Ha ha ha ha . . .'

He was half-way through practising this poor attempt at merriment, when the door of the office opened and his secretary looked in.

'Mr Jack Green to see you, sir,' she said.

The managing director clapped his hand over the chairman's mouth before he could give a scream of panic.

'Show him in,' he said.

Jack's opening words as he came into the office showed just how wrongly Jack had assessed the situation.

'Well, gentlemen,' he said, smiling happily at the two men who faced him, 'I bet you're glad to see me!

The expression on the faces of the two men didn't seem to Jack to bear this out. They looked like they had been carved in stone. And miserable stone at that. Maybe they never got all my message, thought Jack. Well, they'll soon cheer up when they hear what I've got to say.

'About this missing formula . . .' he began.

That was as far as he got.

'Formula?' snarled one of the men. 'We don't know anything about a formula!' And then he turned to the other man, who seemed immensely nervous, for confirmation. 'Do we?' he barked.

The other man mopped his head.

'A missing formula?' the nervous man repeated hollowly, and then he began to laugh in a most bizarre mechanical way. 'Ha ha ha ha . . .'

Then, before Jack's eyes, he suddenly stopped laughing, turned a funny grey colour, and fell off his chair on to the floor where he lay moaning. Jack leapt to his feet, concerned. Was the man ill?

'Are you all right?' asked Jack, but before he could reach the man on the floor the other man leapt in front of him.

'Don't you touch him, you swine!' he snarled.

'Eh?' said Jack, completely baffled.

'You think you're clever, don't you!' snarled the man. 'Well, we haven't got any missing formulae missing, so there, and even if we had they would be nothing to do with us! So get out!'

Jack stared at the man bewildered.

'Out!' snapped the man again, and this time he opened the door to give Jack an even clearer idea of what he wanted Jack to do.

Jack shook his head and went towards the door. As he did so he was relieved to see that the other man was getting up off the floor, even if he did still look a little grey in the face.

'Well, nice to have met you,' said Jack politely, still wondering why the two men were so upset.

The really angry man still wasn't finished with Jack.

'Just because you appear on TV. . . !' he snarled at him accusingly.

Jack was pleased at the change of subject matter. Maybe this would steer the conversation around to something they could talk about without arguing.

'Actually I'm on again tomorrow. Lunchtime, BBC 1 . . .' he began cheerfully.

The angry man obviously didn't want to know.

'Get out!' he shouted, pointing in the direction of Out.

Jack took the hint. He went.

It was only after he'd gone and the door had shut behind him that the managing director and the chairman realized what Jack had said.

'He's appearing on TV tomorrow!' screamed the managing director. 'He's going to tell everyone about our gas! Quick, the phone! Get me MI5!'

CHAPTER SEVEN

The Beard

The next morning Jose Cuervo sat in his bed-sitter, holding Miss Taylor's letter and pondering the problem of how to get the formula for the Death Gas back.

'There *must*-a be a link between this Jack Green and this Winfield School,' he mused to himself. He wondered if maybe this man Green was a teacher there? There was only one way to find out and that was to go back to the school. And just in case this Miss Taylor or that little girl saw him again. . . ! Cuervo opened a drawer of his dressing table and took out a big, bushy false beard and put it on. There! Now no one would recognize him!

* * *

At the school Jack and the headmaster were walking across the playground.

'The TV crew are all ready for you in Mr Hammond's room,' said the headmaster. 'I've arranged for some children to be there.'

'I really must thank you for your co-operation in using the school for this,' said Jack. 'After all, not many head teachers would want their school to appear on TV as having contaminated water.'

Hearing this, the headmaster almost stopped in his tracks. Contaminated water! Good Lord, he hadn't thought of that! He'd just thought what a feather in the school's cap this being featured on television was. And especially with the new School Inspector, Mr Winters, coming to visit the school today as well. He'd thought it would be something to boast about!

'Mind,' continued Jack, cheerfully oblivious of the headmaster's sudden concern, 'all the drinking water in this country is in a terrible state, even though we spend a fortune trying to clean it. Did you know that every time someone in London drinks a glass of water, nine other people have drunk that same glassful of water before them?'

Nine other people! thought the headmaster. Ugh!

'That's why we have to stop people and companies polluting the water in the first place,' said Jack. 'Which is why this TV interview is so important. It will highlight the fact that there is a problem, and hopefully force the authorities to do something about it.'

'Yes,' said the headmaster, now wondering how much it would cost him to drink bottled water. 'Er, Mr Green, these nine other people who've drunk the water before me . . . Might I know them?'

As they neared the school building Jack and the headmaster were unaware that they were being shadowed by a lollipop lady. This was Dorothy Greckle in disguise, carrying out her orders to shadow this man Green, and stop him giving the TV interview. There seemed to be only one way to do this.

Much as she hated to hurt anyone, her plan was to get Jack on his own, and then bash him over the head with the lollipop stick.

Unknown to Dorothy, Butch Brooks and Georgio

Nitzkov also had orders to stop Jack from giving the TV interview, and, coincidentally, both men had arrived at the school disguised as pest controllers. Even now they were glaring at each other in the corridor.

'Listen,' snarled Butch, 'I don't know how you KGB characters . . .'

'I am not KGB!' hissed Georgio. 'I am NFRSS.'

'I don't care if you're an OBE, this guy Green is *mine* and my orders are to stop him.'

Before Georgio could argue they were both aware of voices drawing nearer, and they realized that Jack was approaching the entrance to the school building. Immediately the two men stationed themselves on either side of the double swing doors, ready to pounce on Jack as soon as he stepped through. Unfortunately for them, the caretaker had only just that morning oiled the hinges of the double swing doors, and as Jack and the Head came through, giving the doors a push, the doors swung back with such force that they crashed into Butch and Georgio, smacking each of them on the nose. Jack and the Head continued on their way, unaware of Butch and Georgio sliding unconscious to the floor behind them.

So it was that when Dorothy came in through the doors a few seconds later in her pursuit of Jack, she was astonished to find what appeared to be two pest controllers lying dazed on the floor.

'Good grief!' she gasped.

Butch opened one eye groggily, and found himself looking up at a woman clutching what appeared to be an outsized lollipop. Then his vision cleared and he recognized her. It was that MI5 agent!

His memory wasn't exactly clear as to what had happened. All he remembered was the door opening, and then that bash on the nose. He staggered to his feet and glared at Dorothy.

'So!' he snarled. 'You did it, huh!'

'Did what?' asked Dorothy, bewildered. Nearby, Georgio lurched to his feet, rubbing his injured nose. Georgio blinked his eyes, and then saw Dorothy holding the lollipop stick. As he watched he saw Butch move forward suddenly, grab Dorothy and start to bundle her towards a door marked 'Stock Room'.

Dorothy was astonished by this sudden turn of events. What on earth did this man think he was up to? He must think that *she* had hit him with her lollipop stick! Good Lord! She tried to push him away so that she really could hit him with it, but he was too near for her to get a good swing. She was desperately trying to remember the karate training she'd received at Secret Agent School, when she heard a voice from further along the corridor calling: 'What's going on?!'

Dorothy, Butch and Georgio looked round, and there was the headmaster, on his way back from having delivered Jack to the TV crew and astonished to find two pest controllers apparently trying to push a lollipop lady into the Stock Room.

Butch weighed up the situation and realized there was only one course of action open to him. He ran out of the doors and headed for the school exit. Georgio rubbed his nose, also weighed the situation up, and came to the same decision. He was just a few seconds behind Butch as they rushed out of the door.

By now the headmaster was beside Dorothy.

'Are you all right?' he asked, baffled.

Dorothy gave him a smile.

'Absolutely,' she said. 'All in a day's work. Ah well, back to the job.'

And with that, she too went, leaving the headmaster to ponder over the fact that the population seemed to be getting more lunatic with each passing day.

* * *

While all this was going on, Jack had been in Mr Hammond's classroom practising for his interview while the TV crew checked sound levels, lights, camera angles, and all the other paraphernalia that went with a TV interview. Finally, everything was now ready. A row of children had been hand-picked to provide a backdrop for Jack, their ages ranging from nine to thirteen, and they all now stood behind Jack, beaming happily at the camera.

Jack held out a glass of water towards the camera.

'This is a glass of water,' he announced for those viewers who didn't immediately recognize it as such. 'It came from a tap in this school. The children behind me here drink this water. This water contains lead, aluminium, nitrates, pesticides and, worst of all, a liquid used for cleaning diesel engines, called trichloroethylene.'

During Jack's speech, as he listed the constituents of the water, the children's smiles had begun to fade, and now, as he named this last of all, one little girl's face crumpled completely and she let out a wail: 'Waaaaahhhh!!'

Jack turned, surprised.

'What's up?' he asked. 'Did I frighten you?'

'Cut!' snapped the director.

Outside the classroom, Michael and Kate had their noses pressed against the window of the door, watching it all. Michael grinned broadly.

'Poor old Uncle Jack!' he chuckled. Then, something moving further along the corridor caught his eye, and he turned to see what it was. The next second he pulled Kate into a hiding place in a nearby alcove.

'What. . .? !' began Kate, startled.

'Ssssh!' whispered Michael, putting his hand over Kate's mouth to shut her up. 'That man's back!'

Kate peered out of the alcove along the corridor. Sure enough, there was Jose Cuervo prowling along the corridor. Admittedly he wore a big bushy beard, but the effect he'd had on them the day he'd nearly driven off with them had made sure that the children would always recognize him, no matter what disguise he wore.

The children followed Cuervo as he crept along, making sure all the while that he didn't turn and spot them. They watched him stop at the door of the headmaster's office. As they watched, Cuervo knocked at the door and they heard the headmaster call 'Come in!'

The headmaster got up from behind his desk as the door opened and the man with the big bushy beard came in. The headmaster smiled and held out his hand.

'Welcome to Winfield Middle School,' he said. 'You must be Mr Winters.'

Cuervo hesitated. Mr Winters? Then, never one to miss an opportunity, he smiled.

'Yes,' he said. 'That is who I am.'

'Right,' said the headmaster, and he indicated the papers he had laid out on his desk.

'I've got these all ready for you. This is our plan for the National Curriculum as far as science is concerned . . .'

'Oh, good,' beamed Cuervo, not having the faintest idea what this man was talking about. Before the headmaster could enlarge on this 'National Curriculum', Cuervo asked him: 'Before we go on, do you happen to know where I could find a Mr Jack Green?'

Outside the headmaster's office Kate and Michael had been listening, and they now stared at each other in horror.

'He's after Uncle Jack!' said Michael. 'We've got to do something. . . !'

'We'd better call the police,' suggested Kate.

Michael shook his head.

'There's no time for that,' he said. 'Maybe we could tell Uncle Jack?'

'Not in the middle of his TV interview,' pointed out Kate.

They frowned, thinking hard, and then they both had the same thought together.

'Miss Taylor!' they said in unison.

Miss Taylor was on her way along the corridor when, as she turned a corner, Kate and Michael ran straight into her. Miss Taylor staggered back and glared at the two children.

'Kate and Michael!' she said. 'How many times must I tell you about running in the school. . . !'

'Miss Taylor,' blurted out Michael urgently, 'that man's back and he's in the head's office!'

'What?!' said Miss Taylor, stunned. 'The nerve of

the man! Does he think he can come in here unrecognized?!'

'He's in disguise,' said Kate. 'He's got a big false beard on.'

'Has he?!' said Miss Taylor grimly. 'Right! Leave this to me!'

In the headmaster's office Jose Cuervo had received a serious setback. Before the headmaster could give him the information about this man Green, the door of the office had opened and another big man with a really huge bushy beard – so huge that it made Cuervo's false beard look like a wisp of hair – entered.

'Good morning,' said the bearded man. 'My name's Winters. I'm the new school inspector.'

The headmaster's mouth dropped open and he turned to look at Cuervo. Cuervo gulped, and then thinking quickly he blurted out: 'Wrong school!'

And with that, Cuervo rushed out of the office and out of the school as fast as he could, with the headmaster and Winter looking after him in bewilderment.

'Funny chap!' commented Winters. 'Who was he? A parent, I suppose?'

'Er . . .' said the headmaster. 'Actually, he told me . . .' And then he stopped. He wanted to impress this man Winters, not let him realize that he was the sort of headmaster who couldn't recognize a real school inspector when he saw one. Hastily, he smiled and indicated the papers on his desk. 'May I say what a pleasure it is to welcome you, Mr Winters. Now, if you'd like to look at our schedules for the National Curriculum . . .'

At that moment the door crashed open and Miss

Taylor burst in. She stood framed in the doorway like some avenging angel.

The head blanched.

'Er, this is Miss Taylor, one of our teachers . . .' he said, by way of introduction.

Miss Taylor glared at Winters.

'And I know who you are!' she cried triumphantly.

And with that, she grabbed hold of Winters's big, bushy beard and pulled. His roar of pain was heard all over the school, even as far as Mr Hammond's room, where Jack was half-way through his announcements about water for the fifth time.

The director let out a moan.

'Cut!' she yelled.

CHAPTER EIGHT

Working Together

At the offices of the CIA all was not well. Butch
Brooks stood to attention in front of the desk of his
boss, Herman Shoemaker, listening to Shoemaker
telling him that he was a buffoon, a numskull, a
deadbrain. In short . . .

'You are an idiot, Brooks.'

'Yes, sir,' said Butch.

'An ordinary Joe like this Green Guy,' continued
Shoemaker, 'and you *still* haven't got this formula
off him . . .'

'He is a tricky . . .' began Butch.

'Shut up!' said Shoemaker. 'I don't want excuses,
I want that formula. And I want it in twenty four
hours!'

'Yes, sir,' said Butch.

'Then don't just stand there. Go and get it.'

Shoemaker watched as Butch saluted smartly and
then marched towards the door. Give me strength!
groaned Shoemaker. How can I run a Secret Service
outfit with morons like that?!

Butch was just about to go out, when Shoemaker
suddenly remembered something he had meant to
tell him.

'There's one more thing, Brooks!' he called.

Butch stopped. Maybe Mr Shoemaker was going
to tell him he wasn't an idiot after all?

'Yes, sir?' he said hopefully.

'I forgot to tell you, we've got a whole new bowl of beans opening up on this case. You know these talks going on in Geneva between our guys from the State Department and the Russkies. . . ?'

'Yes, sir,' said Butch. (He didn't know, but he thought it was best to let his boss think he was up-to-date on information.)

'Well, from now on we're all working together.'

Butch stared at his boss goggle-eyed.

'Working together?! But. . . !'

'I know,' said Shoemaker ruefully, 'but that's the way it is. From now on you and this Russki guy, Georgio Nitzkov, are partners. And those are orders from Washington. Got it?'

Partners with Nitzkov! Butch could scarcely believe his ears! However, if that's what his boss was telling him, that's the way it would be.

'Yes, sir,' he said, and he went.

Shoemaker sat looking at the closed door for a few seconds. He wondered if in fact the door had more intelligence than Brooks? And on top of all that, to be working with the Russkies! The world was sure changing fast, that was for certain. He pondered over it for a minute more, weighing the situation up. He had to face the facts, his CIA agent on this case was a klutz. If he, Herman Shoemaker, was going to get that formula back without the Russkies ripping him off, then he had to call in a professional. Okay, it would cost money, but it had to be done for the Safety of the World. And in all the world there was only one professional mercenary who was up to this job.

His decision made, Shoemaker reached for his

phone, dialled a number, and when it answered said, in a cautious whisper: 'Hello? Is that The Vixen?'

* * *

At the offices of the NFRSS, Georgio Nitzkov was suffering a similar fate to Butch Brooks, at the hands of his NFRSS Controller, Mikhael Rinzikov.

'You are an idiot, Nitzkov!' said Rinzikov, concluding a long list of other names which he had called Georgio during the last fifteen minutes.

'Yes, Comrade,' said Georgio.

'You have disgraced the name of the NFRSS! I want that formula! And I want it in twenty four hours! Now go and get it!'

Georgio was about to say 'Yes, Comrade' again, when he decided against it – it might only give his superior another chance to call him names. Far better to keep his mouth shut and just head for the door. He was almost at the door when Mikhael Rinzikov called him back. Oh no, more names! groaned Georgio; but he was wrong.

'There is one more thing I have to tell you.'

'Yes, Comrade?' asked Georgio.

Rinzikov sighed, almost mournfully.

'We also have a whole new bowl of borscht opening up on this case. You know there are talks going on in Geneva between our people from the Kremlin and the Yankees. Well, from now on we're all working together.'

Georgio stared at him, shocked.

'Working together?! But. . . !'

'Those are the orders from Moscow. From now on, you and this Yankee, Bootch Brooks, are partners. Right, Nitzkov?'

Georgio gulped. Partners with a Yankee? Amazing!

He nodded.

'Yes, Comrade,' he said.

After Georgio was gone, Rinzikov sat at his desk, brooding. It was bad enough that they should be working with the Yankees, but to be saddled with this Nitzkov, this . . . this bonehead! No, if he, Mikhael Rinzikov, was going to get that formula back without the Yankees ripping him off, then he had to call in a professional. Okay, it would cost money, but it had to be done for the Safety of the World. And in all the world there was only one professional mercenary who was up to this job.

His decision made, Rinzikov reached for his phone, dialled a number, and when it answered said in a cautious whisper: 'Hello? Is that The Vixen?'

* * *

Kate and Michael were fed up. They sat in their living room, being officially 'minded' by Uncle Jack while their mum and dad were out at a Bank 'do'. They were telling Jack just how fed up they were because they'd got into serious trouble at school over the beard-pulling incident.

'And Miss Taylor blamed *us*!' said Kate, indignantly. 'Just because she's too thick to spot a real spy.'

'And if you ask me it's all your fault, Uncle Jack,' complained Michael.

'Mine?' queried Uncle Jack, defensively.

'Yes,' expanded Michael. 'If that man hadn't been chasing after you, none of this would ever have happened.'

'Get it right, Michael,' said Uncle Jack. 'If he hadn't stolen this formula from the chemical company in the first place . . .'

'But they told you the formula wasn't theirs,' Kate pointed out.

'If it is a formula,' said Michael.

Jack frowned. That was the one thing that still puzzled him. It certainly looked to him like a chemical formula. Then he had an idea.

'I know!' he said.

Michael and Kate looked at him.

'There's one way to find out whether it *is* a chemical formula or not. I've just remembered an old friend of mine: Cynthia Birdwood. She used to lecture in physics and chemistry when I was at university. She was absolutely brilliant. A genius. A bit eccentric, though.'

'Huh!' commented Michael. 'Hark who's talking!'

Jack took out the piece of paper with the formula on it and looked at it again.

'I'll give this to her,' he said. 'She'll soon know if it's a chemical formula or not. In fact, I'll get her to make some of it, whatever it is.' He grinned at Michael and Kate, pleased that now he had a plan. 'One sniff of whatever it is and we'll soon find out what all this fuss is about!'

CHAPTER NINE

Enter The Vixen

Jack sat in the living room in Cynthia Birdwood's
tiny cottage. He was doing his best to avoid being
smothered by her various cats, who seemed intent
on using him as a cushion to sleep on, while Cynthia
studied the piece of paper that Jack had just given
her.

'Well it looks like a gas of some sort,' said
Cynthia, at last.

'What sort?' asked Jack.

'Hard to tell at this stage,' said Cynthia. 'Some
sort of amino acids. By the way, you're not sitting on
Harold, are you?'

Jack looked down at the cushions of the settee he
was on.

'Harold?' he asked.

'A Persian tabby. He usually sits on that settee.'
As Jack began to search the cushions, looking
slightly alarmed, moving the other cats as he did so,
Cynthia grinned. 'Don't worry, if he was there you'd
soon notice. He'd stick his claws in your bottom.'
And she gave a chuckle. 'He did it to the vicar last
week. Poor man nearly went through the ceiling.'

Jack settled down on the settee once more,
dislodging a slothful-looking Manx cat.

'Getting back to the formula,' he said. 'Do you
think you'll be able to make it up?'

'I can't see why not,' said Cynthia, confidently.

76

She tucked the piece of paper behind an ornamental vase on her mantelpiece and just managed to stop a large ginger tom from sneaking on to her armchair before she could sit down. 'For one of your "green" campaigns, is it?'

'I don't know yet,' said Jack. 'That's why I want to find out what it is. The chemical company I thought it had been stolen from deny all knowledge of it.'

Cynthia shook her head doubtfully.

'It's bound to be something nasty, then,' she said. 'You can take my word for it, after fifty years spent working in science, anything that people deny all knowledge of usually is. *You've* no idea what it does, have you?'

'None at all,' said Jack. 'All I know is, whatever it is, the man who dropped it is desperate to get hold of it.'

* * *

Another man who was also desperate to get hold of the formula was at that very moment giving Dorothy Greckle a dressing down.

M paced about his office, hands clasped behind his back in a military manner, while Dorothy stood to attention. M was not happy.

'I had the managing director of Gaschem on the phone to me for half an hour demanding to know what we are doing about getting the formula back,' he stormed, still pacing. 'Remember, this is a formula for the most deadly gas ever invented! This gas disintegrates bones . . .'

'I know, sir,' said Dorothy with a shudder. 'Human jellyfish. You did tell me.'

'And what have you done to get it back? Nothing.

78

It's not good enough, Agent 7. Not good enough at all.'

'No, sir,' said Dorothy. She felt miserable. A failure.

'So we're going to have a change of plan,' continued M.

Dorothy's heart sank. She was going to get the sack. Back to the Uniformed Branch. Perhaps even, horror of horrors, a traffic warden! But no. M's next words told her that she was being given another chance.

'You're being given another chance, Agent 7,' he said. 'But bear in mind that I want that formula back from this man Green, and I want it back within forty eight hours. Have you got that?'

'Yes, sir,' Dorothy nodded.

'To do it,' continued M, 'You're going to have to go underground.'

Dorothy shivered at the thought. She hated going underground.

'Do I have to, sir?' she pleaded. 'I much prefer to use buses.'

Not for the first time it crossed M's mind that Agent 7 was not really the right person for this assignment, nor any assignment for the Secret Service.

'I am talking about becoming an undercover spy,' he said, patiently.

'Oh,' said Dorothy.

'You're going to infiltrate. Pretend to be one of him.'

Dorothy frowned, slightly perplexed.

'One of what, sir?' she asked.

'A Greenie, or whatever they call themselves,'

said M. 'This is your equipment . . .'

M went across to a large cupboard and from it began taking out and handing to Dorothy the Regulation Issue 'Green Infiltrator Equipment': badges; banners; an inflatable whale; sandals; chains . . .

As he passed the chains to her, Dorothy hesitated.

'Something wrong, Agent 7?' asked M.

'Yes, sir,' said Dorothy. 'What are the chains for?'

'For chaining yourself up to things, of course. Fences, drilling rigs, bulldozers . . . these Greenies are always doing it.' He continued handing things out to Dorothy. 'A dozen free range eggs . . . a portable rainbow . . .'

Finally, when Dorothy was completely loaded down with her new equipment, M shut the cupboard door.

'There,' he said. 'You're all ready. I've also booked you in for a "Green Training Crash Course" at HQ so you can learn all the jargon. "Eco-friendly washing-up liquid", that sort of thing. You're due there in twenty minutes. By the end of the day you should be a completely believable "Greenie". Then you can go and get to know this man Green, and once you're in his confidence you can snatch back the formula. All clear?'

'Spot on, sir,' said Dorothy.

'Good,' said M. 'Then go and get that formula.'

M watched Dorothy as she staggered out of the office, barely able to walk under the weight of all the equipment. As soon as the door had closed behind her, he picked up his internal telephone and called his immediate superior, Sir Alex Sanderson.

'Alex?' he said. 'Look, I'm worried about our

agent on this business of the formula. Frankly, I don't think she's up to it. Not tough enough. We need a ruthless professional on this if we're going to get that formula back . . . Right . . .' And he nodded gravely. 'My thoughts entirely. Much as I dislike the idea, we're going to have to go out of our own organization. It's going to cost money, but we've got to get hold of this formula before anyone else does.' He nodded again as Sir Alex at the other end of the telephone mentioned a name. 'Yes, that's who I'm talking about: the best crook and freelance spy there is in the whole world. We've got to get The Vixen!'

* * *

The Vixen prided herself on her hide-out, a luxurious apartment hidden away at the top of what looked like a disused warehouse in one of the dingier parts of London. She stood at the window, holding the portable telephone, looking down at the gloomy streets far below. Down there all was drab, dirt-ridden and graffitied, dark and so sad. Here, in her high-ceilinged, white-walled apartment all was luxury: furniture from the most exclusive Italian interior designers, wall coverings form Paris . . . Along the whole of one wall ran an illuminated fish tank, inside which a shoal of piranha fish threshed and fought, biting at something dark and gruesome that lay on the bottom. And dug into the floor, in the very centre of the apartment, was a submerged pond in which lay Cuddles, the Vixen's pet alligator, resting after his lunch.

The Vixen smiled as she listened to the voice of M at the other end of the line.

'And this gas turns people into human jellyfish by melting all their bones?' She smiled. 'How terribly, terribly wonderful. I've been looking for something like that for years. It will make feeding my piranha fish so much easier. Why, only yesterday one of them got a bone stuck in its throat. Poor, sweet thing. I had to give it the kiss of life. Unfortunately' – and she gave a sigh – 'I was just a little too late. But never mind.' And she stroked the now lifeless body of the piranha that dangled from her ear as an earring. 'It's still close to me. All I need is one for the other ear. However, back to business: this formula of yours sounds just too, too wonderful to resist. Of course I'll get it for you, but I'd have thought you'd have had your own agent already on the case?'

'We have,' came M's voice, 'but . . . how can I put it. . . ? The woman's an idiot.'

The Vixen smiled again.

'An idiot?' she echoed delightfully. 'I *love* competing with idiots. You can afford to lose her, can you?'

Something in the Vixen's voice, so sweet, so genteel, made M shiver at the other end of the line. He hated dealing with the Vixen, she was so evil but, in the circumstances, what choice did he have?

'I'd . . . er . . . I'd prefer that she didn't come to any harm,' he said awkwardly.

'Oh, I hope not as well, sweetness,' cooed the Vixen, 'but you know what I'm like if I get a teensy weensy bit cross.'

'One more thing,' said M hesitatingly. 'I know I don't even need to ask this, but . . .'

'Yes?' coaxed the Vixen.

'You will work only for us on this? I mean, I'm not

82

suggesting that you might consider taking money from some other organization . . .'

The Vixen laughed, a soft purring laugh. 'You silly boy!' she said. 'Don't worry, I shall work only for you on this. You know that you can trust me absolutely implicitly. Ciao.'

The Vixen hummed happily to herself as she hung up, and then she tapped out the number of the NFRSS on her portable phone.

'Comrade Rinzikov?' she said, when the phone at the other end was picked up. 'I've been thinking over your request about this gas that melts people's bones. I thought I'd let you know that I'll be delighted to take the job on for you, for a price.'

That done, she replaced the phone while she looked up the number of the CIA.

CHAPTER TEN

Miss Taylor

Uncle Jack walked along the street towards the school gates, fully aware of the large van following him at walking speed. It was hard not to be aware of the van, bristling as it was with aerials like a TV licence detector van. Inside the van he knew were the two 'undercover policemen' he'd spoken to the other day. He knew that because he could just see them through the darkened glass of the van's windows.

Once again he wondered why they were following *him*, when they should have been keeping an eye on Kate and Michael.

The reason Jack was on his way to the school was because he was still concerned about Kate and Michael's safety. Okay, so far there had been no other incidents like the one that day in the van, but you could never be too careful; particularly as the mysterious man had come back to the school.

Jack checked his watch. Three thirty. School should be over in ten minutes. He would wait inside and meet them as they came out of their classrooms.

As Jack turned into the school gates Georgio pulled the van to a halt, and immediately he and Butch climbed into the back. In the back of the van it looked like something out of NASA, with the best radio receiving and transmitting equipment the CIA could provide. Even now, as Butch switched it on, the two spies could hear the click-clack-click-clack of Jack walking along. Butch nodded in satisfaction.

'Those mikes that I stuck in the heel of every pair of his shoes are the best there is. Made in Japan. You can't beat 'em. Listen . . .'

They listened as Jack's heels continued click-clack-click-clack, and then clump-clump-clump up the stairs of the school, and then thud-thud-thud on the wooden floor of the school corridor.

'Don't worry,' Butch assured Georgio. 'So long as he doesn't walk and talk at the same time, we'll be okay.'

'I wonder what he's doing at the school?' mused Georgio. 'Perhaps he stashed the formula here?'

'Maybe he's just going to pick up those two kids?' suggested Butch. Then they heard Jack's voice coming through. 'Ssssh!' said Butch. 'He's talking to someone!'

Inside the school the 'someone' that Jack was talking to was Miss Taylor.

Miss Taylor had, in fact, been thinking about talking to Uncle Jack for some time. Not only about Green issues – the environment, the ozone layer, the rain forests – but about more personal matters. Mr Green, she felt, was a 'champion', but, like many champions, something was lacking in his life. She knew that he'd been married once upon a time, many years ago, that his wife had died and that since then, Jack Green had been a widower, bearing his loneliness, she felt, with great bravery. In her opinion, there was no need for him to continue to bear that solitude any longer. It was fate, she decided, that had brought him in today.

'Why, Mr Green,' she smiled. 'How wonderful to see you!'

Jack returned the smile. He felt that there was always something about Miss Taylor that was a bit overpowering.

'I'm waiting for Kate and Michael,' he explained. 'I'm giving them tea today because I thought it would give their mother a break. I also think Edward was relieved because he's taken the day off to do some work at home – though between you and me, I suspect he's actually going to try to finish his latest matchstick model.'

'See?' said Butch. 'I told you he was going to pick up those two kids. That's because we in the CIA are trained to have hunches.'

'Sssssh!' hissed Georgio. 'I'm trying to listen.'

In the corridor, Jack was suddenly aware that Miss Taylor didn't seem to be saying much; she just gazed at him with an intensity that he found unnerving. He wondered if he had a smudge on his nose. He gave her a smile.

'Anyway,' he said chattily, 'how are you?'

'Mr Green . . .' said Miss Taylor. Jack saw that she really did look deadly serious, and for a moment he wondered whether something awful had happened to Kate or Michael.

'Are Kate and Michael all right?' he asked.

'What?' said Miss Taylor, slightly thrown by this question.

She dismissed the subject of the childen with a wave of her hand. 'Fine, fine,' she said. Then she adopted her serious look again. 'Mr Green, I know that a man like you must feel so dreadfully alone
. . .'

Oh-ho, thought Jack. He had a sinking feeling what was coming. A man alone. A man needing to be looked after. He looked at his watch, but it offered no escape, there was still two minutes to go before the bell for the end of school.

'Actually . . .' he began, but Miss Taylor ignored his words.

'You are a man with a mission. A man who now and then must yearn for some peace. A man who says to himself "If only I had some arms . . ." '

'I've got two!' pointed out Jack with a smile, making a joke of it.

'Some arms to fall into,' added Miss Taylor, just in case he'd missed what she meant.

'Ah . . .' said Jack, not sure of what else to say.

'Mr Green,' continued Miss Taylor, passionately, 'I sometimes think that you have been alone too long.'

'I don't think of myself as alone,' countered Jack.

'People who are alone never do,' said Miss Taylor. 'What you need is a stable companion . . .'

'A horse, you mean?' asked Jack.

Miss Taylor was beginning to get slightly irritated by Jack's responses. It was almost as if the man was deliberately misunderstanding her.

'Someone in a stable job,' she said. 'Like teaching, for example.'

Inside the van, Georgio gave a squawk.

'She's asking him to marry her!' he yelled.

'Shuttup!' bellowed Butch. 'I wanna know what he answers!'

The two spies leaned forward intently, ears almost glued to the radio receiver, listening as Miss Taylor's voice came loud and clear through to the receiver in the back of the van.

'Mr Green, you may see before you just a quiet and shy person . . .' came Miss Taylor's voice, and then vanished to be replaced by the sounds of music.

'What the. . . ?' yelled Butch.

'You've lost them!'

Frantically, Butch twiddled the knobs and banged the dials, but all to no avail. They searched the frequencies of the airwaves and picked up the AA, the RAC, various CB freaks, taxi drivers, and nearly every radio station in the Northern hemisphere, but the conversation between Miss Taylor and Uncle Jack had gone.

Actually, Butch and Georgio hadn't really missed much, because just as Miss Taylor was getting really intense, the bell went for the end of school and Kate and Michael appeared.

'Hello, Uncle Jack,' said Kate cheerfully. 'All ready for tea. Goodnight, Miss Taylor.'

Miss Taylor forced a smile at the two children, but in her heart she wished that the bell had been delayed for just a few seconds longer, or that Kate and Michael hadn't been able to find their coats quite so quickly.

'Come on, children,' said Uncle Jack. 'Nice talking to you, Miss Taylor.'

And with that, Jack and the two children went. Behind them, watching them go, Miss Taylor stood enthralled, her hands clasped together.

He said 'nice talking to me!' she enthused silently. He likes me!

CHAPTER ELEVEN

Hostages

Jose Cuervo had not been idle. He had sat himself down in the local library to leaf through the back numbers of the local paper, searching for any news stories that might have appeared about anyone called Jack Green. Luckily for him, he did not have to look far: nearly every other edition seemed to carry a photo or a story about this man Jack Green. As far as Cuervo could tell, the man was an interfering busy-body and if he had lived in San Perdino under the rule of El Presidente Generalissimo San Carlos Perdita San Maria Jose Cuervo, then he would have had a very short life indeed.

However, from the newspaper stories Cuervo now had the information he needed: Jack's address: Flat 3, 26 Ashburnham Gardens. So it was that, while Jack was at the school collecting Kate and Michael, Cuervo was hard at work ransacking Jack's flat in a desperate search for the formula, and finding nothing.

'Caramba y bocillada sagitario!' he swore. 'Where would he hide such a thing?!'

And then his eye fell upon a photograph on Jack's wall. The photo showed Jack with Kate, Michael, Elizabeth and Edward.

'Of course!' he cried. 'The little girl! I bet he has hidden the formula at her house!'

It took only a matter of moments for Cuervo to sort

through Jack's desk drawers and find an address book that had another photograph of the Stevens family, with their address written clearly on the back: 12, Pippin Road.

Carefully Cuervo put everything back into the drawers. He did not want this man Green coming home and being alerted by an obvious burglary: he needed to have time to get to this 12 Pippin Road.

As Cuervo slipped out of the entrance to Jack's small block of flats, he did not notice a car parked a few cars behind his battered old van. Nor did he think to check to see if he was being followed as he moved off and headed for 12 Pippin Road.

At the wheel of the car that tailed Cuervo's battered old van, the Vixen gave a little laugh and fingered the elegantly curved ornament that hung from the chain around her neck. She only had to give one sharp tug and the curved ornament became a boomerang with a razor sharp edge. Her favourite weapon, she could slice a blade of grass in half lengthways at 200 metres. She didn't think she would need it against such an oaf as this mysterious burglar, but one never knew.

* * *

Jack was just serving up some more of his home-made carrot cake to Kate and Michael, when his doorbell rang.

'I wonder who that can be?' he said.

'Only one way to find out,' pointed out Michael through a mouthful of carrot cake.

'True,' agreed his uncle, and he went to open the door.

On the doorstep stood a woman whose clothing

93

seemed to consist solely of badges:– badges urging people to Save the Whale, badges warning of the dangers of acid rain, badges of every kind and description. Jack assumed she was collecting for a charity and was already dipping into his pocket, when she said:

'Mr Jack Green?'

'Yes?' said Jack.

'My name's Dorothy Greckle and I'm new to this area. You may not know it, but I'm a Green activist and the thing is, where I come from your name is a legend in the field of environmental activism . . .'

'Is it?' said Jack, a bit taken aback.

'Absolutely,' said Dorothy. 'And when my friends knew I was coming here they said "you must look him up". '

'I see,' said Jack, still a bit stunned. 'Well, Ms . . .'

'Greckle, Dorothy Greckle. Call me Dorothy. The thing is, I want to help you.'

'To do what?' asked Jack.

'To save the planet,' said Dorothy.

'Ah,' said Jack, feeling not for the first time that day a little at a loss for words. 'In that case, perhaps you'd better come in.'

Jose Cuervo pulled up outside 12 Pippin Road and looked at the house. He wondered if he should knock at the door, to find out whether there was anyone at home. The trouble was, if someone answered the door they would recognize him as the most likely suspect once they'd found the house had been burgled. No, he would have to break in and creep around quietly in the house while he searched for the formula. Then, if he was caught by anyone, he would just pull out the huge Magnum gun from his shoulder holster and that would keep them quiet.

Cuervo scanned the house. There was an upstairs window open, close by where the drainpipe ran down the wall. It would take a matter of minutes for someone as fit and agile as Generalissimo San Carlos Perdita San Maria Jose Cuervo to climb up the drainpipe and then in through the window, and then to creep through the upstairs of the house, searching all the bedrooms, as noiselessly as a cat.

Cuervo left his van and went towards the house. In her car, parked a few cars back from Cuervo's, the Vixen watched.

Edward Stevens sat at the living room table and stuck yet another match in place. Piece by piece his model of Big Ben was nearly there. Just the intricacies of the clock face, and then the top to put on, and it would be finished.

He was glad that Jack had offered to give Kate and Michael tea today. Perhaps with this patch of peace and quiet in his otherwise noisy life, he might even begin to draw up the plans for the Taj Mahal as well!

Elizabeth Stevens sat on the settee, worrying. Really, she thought, something had to be done about her brother Jack. At first she had just put all this environmental stuff down to a new hobby that he had taken up. Yes, she agreed with him, and certainly the protection of the planet was of vital importance, but if only Jack didn't have to be so . . . so . . . blatant about it. So outrageous. So unorthodox. Especially with Edward due for a promotion.

'Do you know, Edward,' she said, 'I seriously wonder sometimes if it wouldn't be best for all of us – and, of course, I'm only thinking of Kate and Michael here – if Jack emigrated?'

Edward nodded, not really listening. Nodding was all right; he could nod and still stick matches in place with great care; it was when he talked and tried to do it at the same time that the matches ended up drying in funny positions.

'After all,' his wife continued, 'he's always going on about the Third World and the rain forests and things; maybe we could persuade him to go there, where he's really needed . . .'

A loud crashing noise from upstairs made her stop. She looked at Edward, a worried expression on her face.

'What on earth was that?' she asked.

It was, in fact, Jose Cuervo. His intention to crawl in through the upstairs window and then creep around as quietly as a cat had hit an obstacle. As he had crawled in through the window of the spare bedroom he had slipped and crashed to the floor, and that was the noise that Elizabeth and Edward had heard.

Cuervo stumbled to his feet and took a step backwards, to recover his balance. As he did so, he caught his left foot in a wastepaper basket. He tried to kick it off, but without success. However, the force he used in trying to kick the basket off caused him to stumble. Frantically, he reached out for something to hold on to, and his fingers clutched at a fishing net that was trailing from the top of a wardrobe. (This was, after all, the spare bedroom, where everyone had been depositing junk and bric-a-brac for many years.) The next second the fishing net and a whole load of other junk that was on top of it came crashing down on Cuervo's head.

Downstairs in the living room Elizabeth and Edward listened, transfixed, to the crashing and bashing going on upstairs. Elizabeth looked at Edward.

'I think it's a cat,' said Edward hopefully. 'It must have got in somehow.'

Elizabeth shook her head.

'I think there's someone upstairs!' she whispered.

Edward had to admit, so did he. He turned back to his model of Big Ben, so nearly finished. Perhaps it's just a pigeon, he prayed.

Elizabeth watched him, disappointed by his lack of action.

'Aren't you going to do something?' she demanded.

Upstairs, Cuervo was in even worse trouble. The fishing net had now wrapped itself around him completely, and had also caught in the ornamental handles of a chest of drawers. All pretence at being a noiseless cat had now been abandoned. Desperately, Cuervo gave a hard tug at the net in an attempt to try to free it from the chest of drawers handles; and free it did indeed become. The problem was, Cuervo had pulled with such force that the freeing of the net from the chest of drawers meant that he went flying backwards across the spare bedroom at a great speed. He had slowed somewhat by the time he stumbled through the door and backwards on to the landing, but by then it was too late for him: he was at the top of the stairs.

Cuervo made one last, desperate effort to regain

his balance, his arms whirling frantically like some human windmill, and then he toppled over and crashed backwards down the stairs with thud after thud and a loud yell as he hit the bottom.

'Aaaarghhh!!' came his cry, and even Edward had to admit that this was neither a cat nor a pigeon.

Elizabeth opened the door of the living room and found Jose Cuervo just as he was staggering to his feet and wrenching off the now torn fishing net, which was decorated with sundry other pieces of junk from the spare room.

'What on earth. . .? !' she began.

She didn't get the chance to say much more because Cuervo reached inside his coat and, instead of his Magnum gun, mistakenly pulled out a pen.

'Shut up!' bellowed Cuervo.

Elizabeth, convinced that the pen was a secret weapon of some kind, backed into the living room. Cuervo followed her, his eyes glaring angrily. At the table Edward got to his feet as he saw Elizabeth backing in, and then Cuervo coming in after her.

'Careful, Edward!' gulped Elizabeth. 'He's got a pen!'

'Who . . . who are you?' asked Edward, bewildered.

'Never mind who I am!' snarled Cuervo. 'Where's-a the formula?!'

Elizabeth and Edward looked at each other, baffled.

'Formula? What formula?' asked Edward.

Suddenly Elizabeth shouted out: 'Help! Police!'

'Shut up or I kill you!' bellowed Cuervo. Then an evil smile crossed his face. 'Never mind,' he said, 'I will soon get-a the formula from this man-a Green, now I have-a his sister and brother-in-law as my hostages.'

'Hostages?' said Elizabeth, alarmed.

'Shut up!' snarled Cuervo again. 'Get outside. We are going for a ride.'

Edward looked helplessly towards his model of Big Ben. So near, and yet so far. Perhaps this man would let him take it with him and he could finally finish it. He pointed towards it.

'My model . . .' he began.

Cuervo looked at Edward's nearly-completed matchstick model, and snorted scornfully.

'Ha!' he said.

And with that, he stepped towards the model with one arm raised, ready to bring his fist crashing down on it. Unfortunately, his foot caught in the edge of the carpet and he tripped forward with a yell.

'Aaaargh!!' he went, and he fell face forward on to the table. The effect was the same as if he'd hit it. The model disintegrated in a cloud of flying matchsticks.

Edward and Elizabeth stared at Cuervo and the ruined model in horror. Before they could do something such as leap upon him and overpower him (not that they were thinking of doing any such thing) the Generalissimo scrambled hastily to his feet.

'Out!' yelled Cuervo, gesturing with the pen towards the door. 'Go!'

And with that Elizabeth and Edward raised their hands in the air and half-ran out of the house and across the road to Cuervo's waiting van, Cuervo following closely behind.

In her car the Vixen smiled delicately, but with real pleasure, at this turn of events.

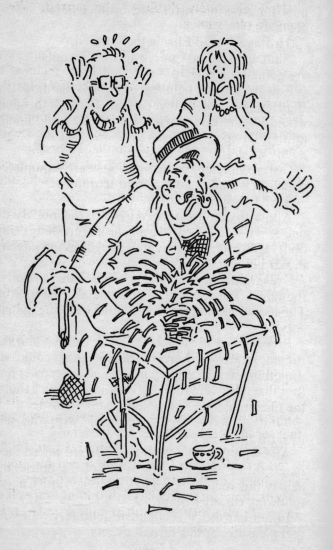

'How absolutely thrilling!' she purred. 'We're going to play games!'

* * *

Kate's and Michael's faces had been pictures of amazement when Dorothy had walked into the flat behind their uncle, but a sharp glare from Uncle Jack had shut them up before they could say anything rude. Uncle Jack could see only too clearly that Michael was thinking 'Another lunatic!'

'These are my nephew Michael and my niece Kate,' Jack had said by way of introduction. 'Michael and Kate, this is Dorothy Greckle.'

From that moment on, the time had been spent with Dorothy enthusing about Jack's 'green' activities and how keen she was to do something to help, and what a lovely flat it was and could she look over it? It was in the middle of all this that the phone rang.

'I expect that's your mum to ask when you're coming home,' said Jack, and he picked up the phone. '4468.'

The voice at the other end of the line was harsh and had a distinctly foreign accent.

'Is that Jack-a Green?'

'Speaking,' said Jack.

'Good. Then listen to me. I have-a your sister and-a your brother-in-law, and unless you give-a me that formula, they will die. Understand?'

'What?' Jack was stunned. 'Who are you. . . ?'

'Never mind who I am. I want-a that formula. I will phone you later to give you instructions.'

With that, Cuervo replaced the phone and walked away from the phone booth, a broad smile on his face. He had done it!

He turned the corner and walked towards where he had parked his van . . . and then stopped. His van had gone!

CHAPTER TWELVE

Dorothy Tells All

Jack watched Kate and Michael's faces as he told them what the man on the phone had said. Their lower lips trembled a bit and they had looked frightened at the terrible news, but Jack reflected that anyone who looked at *him* would notice that *his* lower lip was trembling slightly and that he was also frightened. His fear was for the safety of Edward and Elizabeth, and his lip was trembling because he was so enormously angry with this mysterious man who had kidnapped Kate and Michael's parents.

Dorothy broke the awkward silence.

'What are you going to do?' she asked Jack.

'There's only one thing I can do,' said Jack. 'Give the formula to this bloke and hope we can trust him to hand back Elizabeth and Edward.'

'You mustn't!' said Dorothy.

The conviction in her voice was so strong as she said this that Jack, Kate and Michael all looked at her in astonishment.

'Why not?' demanded Kate.

'I suppose you think we ought to go to the Police,' said Michael. 'Well, we went to them before and it didn't help. And they're *our* parents.'

'I know,' said Dorothy, 'but the reason you mustn't give that man that formula is because . . .'

And here Dorothy stopped, her eyes looking ashamed.

103

'Because of what?' prompted Uncle Jack.

'Because that formula makes a deadly, killer gas.'

Jack and the children stared at Dorothy in astonishment.

'What are you talking about?' asked Jack. 'How do you know that?'

Dorothy hesitated, and then she admitted everything. M wouldn't be happy with her about it, and she would possibly be sent out as a traffic warden after this, but it wasn't fair that these people should be caught up in all this.

'Because I am not really Dorothy Greckle, Green activist. I work for MI5 and my job is to recover that formula.'

'Gosh!' said Kate, stunned. 'A spy!'

Outside in the street, inside the very smart van with darkened windows which bristled with aerials, Butch and Georgio heard all this and grinned at each other.

After the fiasco at the school over the TV interview, they had managed to break into Jack's flat today while he had been at the school collecting Kate and Michael, and they had managed to hide a microphone underneath his telephone table. Not only did it let them eavesdrop on Jack's phone conversations, they were able to pick up every word that was said in the flat. They listened now as Dorothy continued making her confession to Jack and the two children.

'When you say it's a deadly killer gas, what sort of gas?' asked Jack.

'A gas that disintegrates people's bones,' replied Dorothy. 'In fact it's so powerful that just one whiff of the gas and people's bones fall apart and they turn into human jellyfish.'

'Urgh!' said Kate and Michael together in disgust.

Jack stared at Dorothy, stunned as the full horror of the situation hit him.

'But my friend Cynthia's making that formula up right at this very moment. If she breathes it she'll die!'

With that, Jack rushed for the telephone with such speed that he crashed into the telephone table and knocked it over. Inside the van Butch and Georgio held their ears as their microphone recorded the enormous crash at the closest possible range. As fast as he could, Jack tapped out Cynthia's number, and then held his breath as he waited for the phone at the other end to ring. It didn't ring. Instead there was the unmistakeable single-note drone that meant 'unobtainable'.

Jack slammed down the phone, and once again Butch and Georgio inside the van held their ears in agony as the sound echoed through their headphones.

'It's out of order,' said Jack. Then and there he made a decision. 'Right,' he announced, 'I'm going over there. If I'm lucky, I'll get there in time. If I'm not, and she's already made it . . .'

He left the sentence unfinished, but all of them could imagine Cynthia dead on the floor, a boneless human jellyfish. Even Butch and Georgio in the van exchanged grimaces of revulsion at the thought.

'What shall *we* do, Uncle Jack?' asked Kate.

'You two are coming with me,' said Jack. 'With that man kidnapping your Mum and Dad, I'm going to make sure I keep an eye on you.'

'But what about the kidnapper? He's going to be phoning here!' Michael pointed out.

Uncle Jack swore under his breath. Drat! Michael was right. But he daren't take the chance of leaving Kate and Michael here on their own. Say this mystery man came to the flat while Jack was at Cynthia's and snatched them as well?

'I'll stay here and answer the phone for you,' offered Dorothy.

Kate and Michael regarded Dorothy suspiciously.

'How do we know we can trust her?' sneered Michael. 'After all, she's admitted that she's a spy.'

Jack thought it over quickly.

'That may be the very reason we *can* trust her,' he said. 'Anyway, right at this moment we don't have much choice. Let's go!'

Jack headed for the door, closely followed by Kate and Michael. Just before they went out, he turned back to Dorothy.

'If anything happens, Cynthia's address is Laurel Cottage, Ramsden Way, Ealing,' he said. 'We'll be there.'

Then they went.

Inside the van Butch and Georgio leapt into action.

'The formula's at Ramsden Way, Ealing!' said Butch, scrambling into the front seat of the van. 'Let's go!'

CHAPTER THIRTEEN

One Sniff And . . . !

Jack, Kate and Michael sat in Jack's car, looking towards Cynthia's tiny, picturesque cottage. Jack knew he should be getting out of the car and rushing in, but somehow the thought of what might be inside there held him back. With luck, Cynthia wouldn't yet have had a chance to have made up the gas, but on the other hand . . .

Jack turned to his niece and nephew seated in the back of the car. This was no time for hanging about; things had to be done!

'Right, I'm going in,' he said. 'You two stay here.'

'Say she's made this gas?' said Kate unhappily.

'That's why I don't want you two coming in,' said Jack.

'But *you* might breathe it,' pointed out Michael in exasperation. 'We ought to call the Police.'

'I know,' said Jack, 'but there's no time for that now. I got Cynthia into this, and it's up to me to get her out of it.'

He opened the door of the car and got out. Just before he shut the door he said:

'I'm going to try knocking on the front door first. If there's no answer, I'll go round the back because she usually leaves her back door open. Then I'll go in. Once I've gone in, if I'm not out again in ten minutes, call 999 and tell them what's happened.'

With that, Jack shut the car door and walked up

the path towards the front door of Laurel Cottage.

Meanwhile, some fast driving by Georgio had just allowed Georgio and Butch to get them to Cynthia's cottage ahead of Jack and the children. Georgio was about to open the back door when Butch joined him.

'I heard voices,' said Georgio. 'Are they here?'

Butch nodded.

'The kids are still in the car. Green's at the front door. Let's get in before he does.'

Georgio turned the handle of the back door, and the door swung open. Carefully, Georgio and Butch stepped in and found themselves in Cynthia's kitchen. The kitchen was full of different smells: herbs, baking, pastry-making . . . Georgio sniffed, and then a thought struck him.

'Bootch. . . ?' he said nervously.

'What?' asked Butch, his eyes darting nervously around for any signs of someone lying in the house with no bones.

'This killer gas,' continued Georgio. 'What does it smell like?'

Butch regarded his partner with a puzzled frown.

'How do I know?' he said. 'Anyone who smells it . . .' And Butch drew his finger expressively across his throat. 'Zip!'

Georgio shuddered, then went back to inspecting the kitchen. A large covered saucepan simmering away on the stove caught his eye, and he suddenly realized that he hadn't eaten properly all day. His stomach obviously realized the same thing because it gave a little rumble. Butch, just about to move out from the kitchen into the living room, heard the rumbling sound and turned, in time to see Georgio lifting the lid of the saucepan and bending over to smell the steam rising from it.

Immediately, Butch covered his own nose and mouth with a handkerchief.

'Don't smell it. . . !' he yelled at Georgio through the cloth of his handkerchief.

Georgio looked at him, puzzled.

'What. . . ?' he began . . . And then the full horror of what he had just done struck him. This was the secret gas one sniff of which melted all your bones . . . and he had sniffed it! He clutched his throat, but he knew it was too late! He could feel blackness flowing over him . . . all his bones would be melting . . . With his last breath before he fell unconscious he gave a scream, and then he thudded to the floor.

Butch didn't wait any longer; he didn't want to stand here and see his partner turning into jelly before his eyes, nor did he fancy turning into jelly himself. With two swift strides Butch was at the door of the kitchen and then out into the open air, heading back towards the van.

At the front of the cottage Jack knocked at the door again. It was the third time he had knocked and he knew that, as with the previous two knocks, there would be no answer. All he was doing was putting off the moment when he had to go round to the back of the cottage and go inside, and find out if the worst had happened.

He counted to ten silently, then he took a deep breath and turned to go round to the back door. It was just then that Cynthia arrived home, laden down with shopping bags.

'Jack!' she beamed. 'Well well well! What a pleasant surprise! What are you doing back so soon?'

'Cynthia,' asked Jack urgently, 'have you made up that formula yet?'

Cynthia eyed him askance.

'Give me a chance, Jack,' she said. 'You can't just go into Tesco and get the ingredients for it, you know.'

Jack felt like singing out loud with relief!

'Thank God!' he said, and he picked Cynthia up and gave her an enormous hug. Cynthia looked rather taken aback by this, but as Jack put her back down on the path she was already remembering other urgent situations at other times in other places.

'Mind,' she said thoughtfully, 'I remember when we were rigging up the second nuclear reactor in Windscale – this was in the days when I believed in nuclear power – and we ran out of batteries. We used lemons instead. Did you know. . . ?'

But Jack was already back at the car, opening the door and letting Kate and Michael out. If he had looked up, he would have seen a large, glossy van with darkened windows and bristling with aerials, start up just across the road and then take off at speed, as if the Devil was after it.

Jack, Kate and Michael followed Cynthia into her cottage, Jack ducking down to avoid the low beams that went across the ceiling.

'We found out what that gas does,' said Jack. 'It disintegrates bones.'

'Disintegrates bones, eh?' said Cynthia. 'Terrible.'

'Yes,' said Kate. 'It turns people into human jellyfish!'

'I told you it would be something horrible, didn't I,' said Cynthia, almost pleased that she had been

111

correct. 'Would you like some casserole? You must all be feeling a bit peckish. I've got some on the stove.'

Jack, Kate and Michael exchanged doubtful glances. All this talk about people melting had quite put them off any thoughts of food. Cynthia, meanwhile, had continued into the kitchen, still talking about the irresponsibility of some scientists, when she stopped and they heard her exclaim:

'Good heavens! Look at this!'

The note of astonishment in her voice brought them rushing in, and they looked over her shoulder at the unconscious form of Georgio lying on the kitchen floor.

'It's that policeman!' said Jack, recognizing him at once as one of the two men who had been following him around.

'What's up with him?' asked Kate.

'Is he dead?' asked Michael, slightly awed by the thought. After all, with all this intrigue going on, with deadly gases and spies all over the place, there ought to be a dead body.

Cynthia bent down and examined Georgio.

'No,' she said in answer to Michael's question. 'He's breathing all right. If you ask me, he's just fainted.'

As Jack looked down at the unconscious form of Georgio, a thought suddenly occurred to him. It had been lurking at the back of his mind for some time now, once he had really started to think about the fact that the two policemen had been following *him* instead of Kate and Michael.

'D'you know what I think?' he said.

The other three looked at him, intrigued by the suspicious tone in Jack's voice.

'What?' asked Kate.

'I don't think our friend here is a policeman after all.'

Kate, Michael and Cynthia slowly took this thought in.

'But if he's not a policeman. . . ?' began Cynthia.

'Exactly,' nodded Jack, grimly.

'Exactly what, Uncle Jack?' asked Kate, still not quite sure what was going on, and who Uncle Jack and Cynthia thought the man on the floor was.

'I think he might be able to throw some light on your mum and dad's kidnapping,' said Jack. 'Cynthia, have you got any rope?'

CHAPTER FOURTEEN

The Vixen Makes her Move

In her luxury apartment at the top of the old warehouse, the Vixen was studying a set of photographs she had pinned to a cork board on one wall – photographs of Dorothy, Butch and Georgio, which she had been given by their Secret Service bosses so that she would recognize the three agents; and photographs, that she had secretly taken herself, of the people involved in this case: Jack, Kate, Dorothy, and the mysterious South American who had tried to kidnap the parents of the two children.

Poor man, she thought. He must have been so upset to lose his hostages that way. And, of course, his van. She smiled to herself. Did the taking of the van, she wondered, qualify her as a car thief? She almost giggled at the idea that *she* could be described as a 'common criminal'. Common! What an hysterically wonderful thought!

She turned away from the photographs and stood for a moment, looking at Elizabeth and Edward who were tied back-to-back on two chairs, gags tied around the lower halves of their faces to stop them calling out. Not that there was anyone around to whom they could call, mused the Vixen. Perhaps she would be a little kind to them and remove their gags, at least for a little while? After all, it wouldn't do for them to suffocate. At least, not at the moment, while she had an important use for them.

The Vixen stepped towards Elizabeth and Edward and slipped the gags down from their mouths.

'There,' she cooed softly. 'How are my poor dears? Comfortable?'

Elizabeth snorted indignantly and glared at the Vixen.

'No we are not comfortable at all,' she said. 'Untie us at once or we shall be forced to report you to the police.'

The police? The ghost of a smile played around the Vixen's mouth. Really, who did these people think they were dealing with?

'Oh tut-tut,' said the Vixen softly. 'Hansel and Gretel are upset.'

She was just turning away from the couple, when she noticed Edward nudge Elizabeth, as best he could with his hands tied behind him, and whisper something in his wife's ear. Immediately the Vixen swung round, and Dad sat bolt upright again, aware that this woman was exceedingly dangerous.

'Ah-ha!' hissed the Vixen. 'Secrets! What are you two whispering about?'

Immediately, Elizabeth and Edward tightened their lips. The Vixen fingered the razored boomerang around her neck.

'I would strongly advise you to tell me,' she said.

Elizabeth's and Edward's lips remained sealed. The Vixen gave a small tug at one corner of her necklace and the light metal boomerang came away into her hand. She held it delicately, the light glinting on its blade.

'Do you like flowers?' she asked.

Elizabeth and Edward were surprised by this

116

sudden change of subject. They followed the Vixen's gaze to a row of tall flowers in a box on the ledge of a crescent-shaped window, at the far end of the apartment. The next second, the Vixen's hand gave a small flick and the boomerang flashed across the room, sliced through the stems of four of the flowers as smoothly as a wire through butter, and then returned through the air to the Vixen, who caught it elegantly.

'I could remove your lips in the same way if you don't open them,' she said softly.

Edward gulped, then said: 'I was just saying that you've got the same wallpaper that we were thinking of for our bathroom.'

'And now I've seen it I know I was right not to choose it!' added Elizabeth, spiritedly.

The Vixen shook her head and re-clipped the razored boomerang to her necklace.

'Dear, dear,' she said, 'it seems you're going to be tiresome. It's so rude for guests to be tiresome. Do you know what I do with tiresome guests?'

The Vixen walked over to the ornamental pool in the centre of the floor, and then turned to Elizabeth and Edward.

'This is where Cuddles, my pet alligator, lives,' she said. 'Cuddles loves to play. He plays with my tiresome guests.'

'Wh . . . wh . . . What kind of things does he play with them? asked Edward, nervously.

The Vixen gave a low, throaty laugh and walked over to Edward.

'Oh, I do so like a man with a sense of humour,' she cooed, and she rubbed her hand softly over Edward's hair. 'Tell me, do you like *fish*?'

'Well, I am partial to a bit of cod,' admitted Edward.

'How sweet,' said the Vixen.

Elizabeth felt it was about time she stepped in. It didn't do to get too involved with these criminal types.

'Don't talk to her, Edward,' she said.

The Vixen ignored Elizabeth and continued talking to Edward, moving, as she did so, towards the long, illuminated fish tank that ran along one wall.

'I'd like to tell you about my fish,' she said. 'You see, I studied marine biology, and I *do* like to keep my hand in.'

And with that, the Vixen reached into a bowl and took out something that dripped, and from which Edward and Elizabeth were convinced they could see a bone sticking out. She dropped it into the illuminated tank, and the next second there was a churning in the water as the piranha fish leapt upon the object in a frenzy.

The Vixen turned back to Elizabeth and Edward and gave them a delicate smile.

'Or, at least,' she said, 'someone else's hand.'

Elizabeth and Edward exchanged glances, and each could see that the other had suddenly gone very, very pale indeed. The Vixen laughed.

'I'm such a tease,' she smiled. 'Later, possibly. But first I have a phone call to make. You won't think me rude if I make it while you're in the room, will you?' She picked up her telephone and began to tap out Jack's telephone number. 'After all it does concern you, and I think it's so rude to talk about people behind their backs.'

In Jack's flat, Dorothy sat by the phone and waited, twiddling her thumbs nervously. Calm down, she said to herself. Calm down.

She was thinking about the case, and how different it had turned out from what M had led her to believe. According to M, Jack was a fiend in human form, whose intention was to use the deadliest gas ever invented in order to blackmail the Government in some way, and who was prepared to use any means, and anybody, to achieve those ends. In reality she found Jack to be a nice, decent and honest man who cared for his family, and whose caring went as far as putting himself at risk to save the planet upon which his family, and everyone else, depended for their survival. She hated to be disloyal to M but in this case she thought that M had got it wrong.

She wondered how Jack had got on at Cynthia's, and whether, by now, Jack had also been turned into a human jellyfish. She shuddered in horror at the thought. Poor Jack, and those poor children! If only they. . .

The ringing of the telephone interrupted her thoughts. She snatched it up.

'Hello?' she said.

The Vixen was surprised to hear a woman's voice answer. She looked at her board with the photos on it. Ah, this might very well be the idiot agent that M had told her about: Dorothy Greckle. She decided to have a little fun with the girl.

'Mr Jack Green?' enquired the Vixen.

There was a pause, then Dorothy answered, in the deepest voice she could manage: 'Yes.'

The Vixen laughed.

'Very nice, Dorothy. A wonderful impersonation!

This *is* Dorothy Greckle, I presume? Agent 7 with MI5.'

Before the astonished Dorothy could answer, the Vixen went on. 'When Mr Green returns I would appreciate it if you would give him this message, Dorothy. I have his sister and her husband. If Kate and Michael want to see their parents alive again, then he'd better let me have the formula. If he doesn't . . .' And here the Vixen turned to Elizabeth and Edward and gave them a long smile. 'Then I shall feed them, piece by tiny piece, to my piranha fish.'

And with that, the Vixen licked her lips and hung up the phone.

CHAPTER FIFTEEN

Cuervo Takes a Hostage

At Laurel Cottage Jack, Kate, Michael and Cynthia were in deep debate as to what to do with Georgio, who had now recovered consciousness and had been firmly tied to a chair by Cynthia, using knots she remembered from when she had been in the Women's Royal Paratroop Regiment.

So far, all attempts to question Georgio as to who he was, what he had been doing in the cottage, and the whereabouts of Kate and Michael's parents, had been met with a stubborn resistance. All that Georgio would say was: 'I don't care what you do to me, I will never talk!'

Jack, Kate, Michael and Cynthia huddled together in a small scrum in one corner of the living room, keeping a watchful eye on the bound Georgio, who in turn watched them suspiciously.

'What should we do with him?' whispered Jack, feeling a little helpless in this situation.

'I reckon torture's the only answer,' said Michael, vengefully. 'In this film I saw these Indians had captured this other Indian and they made him talk by tying a horse to each of his arms and legs and threatening to tear him apart!'

Jack looked doubtful.

'For one thing, I doubt if we could get four horses into this living room,' he said. 'And for another, I heartily disapprove of physical violence.'

'I've got an idea,' said Kate. 'Let's try psychological torture. We get a plate and we scrape a fork across it time and time again for hours on end, until in the end the noise will drive him mad and he's bound to talk.'

'That's a potty idea,' objected Michael. 'None of us will be able to stand it either.'

Jack mused on these two suggestions and made a mental note that, when all this was over, he was going to suggest to Elizabeth and Edward that they ought to keep a closer watch on the type of films their two children watched; they obviously gave them wrong ideas.

Then Cynthia clapped her hands together in delight.

'I know!' she whooped.

The others looked at her.

'I've just remembered what we used to do to captured spies when I was in the army!' she said gleefully. 'I know what will make him talk!'

With that, she advanced on Georgio, who did his best to back away from her, but being tied hand and foot to a sturdy wooden chair made that difficult.

'Nothing will make me talk!' Georgio insisted, as Cynthia stood in front of him, flexing her fingers. 'I have been trained in all torture-resistance techniques! I am a man of steel! There is nothing you can do to me that will make me tell you what you want to know! Nothing!'

'Oh no?' said Cynthia, and the next second she had thrust her fingers under his arms and begun to tickle him. That was it! Georgio began to writhe and howl with laughter, his yells filling the whole cottage.

'Stop!' he begged. 'I will tell you anything!'

Cynthia stopped tickling him.

'See?' she said to the others, pleased.

Jack knelt down beside Georgio.

'Right,' he said. 'First: who are you and what are you doing here?'

'I am Georgio Nitzkov and I am working on an operation with the NFRSS and the CIA,' confessed Georgio. 'We are trying to get hold of the chemical formula you took for the deadly gas that disintegrates people's bones.'

Michael and Kate exchanged puzzled glances.

'What's the NFRSS?' asked Michael.

'The Newly Formed Russian Secret Service,' said Georgio, slightly peeved at this question. After all, the announcement of the new organization had been on all the television news' programmes. 'Don't you watch *Newsround*?'

'Where are our mum and dad?' demanded Kate, getting to the heart of the matter.

'I do not know,' said Georgio.

The four looked at each other.

'Okay, Cynthia,' said Jack. 'Tickle him again.'

Cynthia put out her hands towards Georgio, who shrank back from them.

'No!' he begged. 'I swear I do not know!'

Cynthia let her hands drop and turned back to Jack.

'I think he's telling the truth,' she said. 'No one can hold out against a tickle.'

Kate and Michael looked upset.

'But if his lot haven't got them . . .' began Kate, miserably.

Jack put his hand on her shoulder, comfortingly.

'Don't worry, we can still use him to get them back,' he said, confidently.

'How?' asked Michael.

'The NFRSS and the CIA will want him back, so we'll swap him in exchange for their help.' He looked at his watch. 'Look at the time, we've been gone ages. We'd better get back to my flat and see if there's been any news of your parents.'

* * *

Miss Taylor had reached a decision. Jack Green had obviously missed the point of what she had been trying to tell him: that he and she were twin souls, already united in a common cause and who could be united in a personal one – their joint happinesses. She had obviously not been direct enough with him, which was why he had misunderstood what she had been trying to say. No – directness was obviously the only answer! She would go to him and tell him straight out: that he was the man for her and therefore *she* was the woman for him.

With this mission in mind, Miss Taylor mounted the stairs to Jack's flat. She had even brought with her a bunch of flowers, a sure way to a man's heart. She reached the door of the flat and rang the bell.

Inside the flat Dorothy froze. She had been expecting the phone to ring, not the doorbell. Who could it be? Maybe it was those two men who had attacked her at the school and tried to push her into the stock room? Perhaps that vicious woman who had phoned, threatening to feed the children's parents to her dreadful fish, had decided to call at the flat in person? Maybe it was that man who had called before and threatened to kill the children's parents

125

unless Jack gave him the formula? Whoever it was, Dorothy was determined that she would be armed and ready for them. The problem was, she *wasn't* armed.

The doorbell rang again, more insistently this time. Dorothy reached a decision. She hurried to the kitchen, selected the biggest frying pan she could find, then went to the door and opened it.

A woman was standing there, smiling sweetly and holding a bunch of flowers. At the sight of Dorothy the woman's face fell.

'Oh,' said Miss Taylor.

'Yes?' asked Dorothy.

Miss Taylor was slightly disconcerted. Who was this strange woman? Was she just a visitor? In which case, why was she doing such things as cooking for Jack? The fact that she obviously was cooking for him, was quite clear – why else would she be holding a frying pan?

Miss Taylor peered past Dorothy, trying to see into the flat.

'Yes?' asked Dorothy again.

'Is Mr Green here?' asked Miss Taylor.

'Actually, he's not here at the moment,' said Dorothy.

Miss Taylor thought it over, and when she'd finished thinking it over she didn't like the conclusions she reached. Jack Green wasn't in the flat but this woman was. Not only was this woman here, she was cooking, which suggested that she had some sort of relationship with this flat, and therefore with the person who lived in it, namely Jack Green.

Miss Taylor sniffed, expressively.

'I see,' she said, in her coldest possible manner.

'Would you be good enough to tell Mr Green that I called?'

And with that, Miss Taylor turned on her heel and headed for the stairs. Dorothy stared after her. What a strange woman. And she hadn't even said who she was, so Dorothy couldn't tell Jack who had called on him. With that in mind, Dorothy set off after Miss Taylor, forgetting that she was still holding the frying pan. Miss Taylor heard Dorothy's footsteps, turned and then backed away at the sight of Dorothy advancing with the frying pan.

'If you dare lay a finger of that frying pan on me I shall notify the police,' she said sharply.

Dorothy stopped, bewildered.

'But . . .' began Dorothy, helplessly.

It was too late for explanations as far as Miss Taylor was concerned.

'Good day,' she said stiffly, and then proceeded down the stairs and back out into the street, while Dorothy returned to the flat to wonder at this strange encounter.

Miss Taylor was on her way down the stairs as Jose Cuervo drew up in a stolen car outside Jack's flats. Cuervo was furious. Not only had he lost his bargaining power – his two hostages – he had also lost his van. So he had been forced to steal this little car, with which he still found difficulty operating the clutch. Cuervo parked the car a few feet from the kerb and then headed for the entrance to Jack's flats, pulling his huge Magnum gun from his shoulder holster as he did so. The time for patience and cunning, he had decided, was over. He would storm into the flat, hold the gun to Jack's head and demand that he hand over the formula.

As Cuervo walked down the path towards the entrance he saw a woman coming out of the flats, who paused just long enough to throw a bunch of flowers, with some force, into a litter bin, before continuing on her way. As she passed Cuervo she growled:

'That two-timing rat!'

'Beunos dias,' nodded Cuervo politely.

Then the two suddenly stopped as they recognized each other, and at the same instant pointed at the other and cried: 'You!'

Miss Taylor opened her mouth, on the point of yelling 'Police! Help!', but Cuervo gave her no chance. Before she could utter one word he had one hand over her mouth and the other holding the gun, aimed at her head.

'Shuttup!' he grated.

Cuervo thought the matter over quickly. Okay, he could threaten Jack Green now; but he would also have this woman to deal with, which would cause him more problems. Far better to play it safe and go back to his original plan: to get the formula in exchange for a hostage. Okay, he had lost his first two hostages, but Fate and Fortune had been kind and had brought him another. He jabbed Miss Taylor in the back with the gun and bundled her towards his parked car.

'Get in,' he said. 'Any funny business and you die!'

Miss Taylor tensed up as if she was going to resist, but Cuervo pressed the gun harder into her ribs. Miss Taylor sighed resignedly and walked obediently towards the car.

CHAPTER SIXTEEN

The Scream

The Vixen weighed up her plans. Once she had got the formula she would hold a telephone auction for it, she decided, and let MI5, the CIA and the NFRSS bid against each other. One million dollars would be the starting price. That should keep her poor little fishes in food for a while.

She might even consider relocating her headquarters. She had always fancied somewhere a little warmer. California, possibly, or Italy. Perhaps the South of France. Brazil, she had been told, was very warm, but it had far too much jungle in it for her liking.

As she pondered these thoughts she was aware of Elizabeth glaring at her, still tied tightly to the chair.

'You won't get away with this,' said Elizabeth coolly.

'No?' said the Vixen. 'I always have done in the past.'

Elizabeth forced herself to show she wasn't impressed by this woman's air of cool sophisticated evil. She was frightened, certainly, but she wasn't going to let this woman have the pleasure of seeing that.

'I'll have you know,' said Elizabeth defiantly, 'that I'm a member of our Neighbourhood Watch Committee.'

'How terribly exciting,' said the Vixen in her

mocking voice. Then she turned to Edward. 'And how about you, Edward?' she asked.

Edward wasn't able to put on as brave a face as his wife. He was scared and, try as he might, he knew that he was showing it. The sight of those piranha fishes in that tank, and that alligator in the pool in the centre of the floor, was sending cold shivers up his spine.

'Me?' he asked nervously.

'Yes,' cooed the Vixen, coming over to him and stroking a long elegant fingernail down his cheek. 'What are you thinking right at this very moment?'

Edward gulped nervously.

'Actually,' he admitted, 'I was thinking that I'd like a nice cup of tea.'

'Edward!' Elizabeth rebuked him. 'Stop fraternizing with the enemy!'

'I just thought . . .' explained Edward, defensively.

'Of course you did,' agreed the Vixen, sympathetically, 'and refreshments will be served later. Much later. But right now . . .' and she pulled the gag up over Edward's mouth, 'I have to make a little phone call.'

The Vixen then stepped round to Elizabeth and pulled her gag up over the mouth, shutting off her protests.

'I do hate to do this,' she said in mock apology, 'but I'd hate you to be uncouth and call out while I was on the phone. And it might be so tempting.'

With Elizabeth and Edward well and truly gagged, the Vixen picked up her telephone and tapped out Jack's number. He should be back home by now, she mused. And even if he wasn't, that silly

MI5 woman, Dorothy Greckle, could take a message.

Dorothy jumped as the phone rang. As she picked it up she was hoping desperately that it would be Jack or one of the children to say that everything was all right. But it wasn't; it was that woman again, her voice smooth and elegant at the other end of the line.

'Hello again, Dorothy,' purred the Vixen. 'I'd like to speak to Mr Green.'

'He's . . . er . . . not here at the moment,' said Dorothy.

At that moment, behind her, she heard the door of the flat open, and then the voices of Jack and the children calling: 'Hello!'

'He's just come in,' said Dorothy quickly into the phone. Then, covering the mouthpiece, she called urgently to Jack: 'It's her!'

'My sister?' exclaimed Jack.

Kate's and Michael's faces lit up.

Dorothy shook her head. She had forgotten that they didn't know about this new development.

'No,' she said. 'It's a woman who says *she's* got Kate and Michael's parents.'

Jack took the phone from Dorothy, while Cynthia pushed the still tied-up Georgio into the flat and shut the door.

'Hello. . . ?' said Jack into the phone.

'Why, hello, Mr Green,' purred the Vixen. 'Or may I call you Jack? I feel we have so much in common. You are so close to your sister and brother-in-law, and right at this moment, so am I.'

And she smiled at the bound Elizabeth and Edward. The evil menace behind her smile made both Elizabeth and Edward shudder.

132

'Earlier I had a phone call from a man telling me that *he* had got them,' said Jack. 'Why should I believe that *you* have got them now?'

The Vixen gave a little sigh into the phone.

'That's the trouble with the world today,' she said, with an air of mock sadness. 'There's so little trust. Elizabeth, perhaps you'd like to say a few words to your brother.'

The Vixen took the phone over to Elizabeth and lowered her gag.

'Jack, this horrible woman . . . .' began Elizabeth.

That was as far as she got, because, suddenly, the Vixen stamped hard on Elizabeth's foot, and Elizabeth let out a piercing scream all the way down to the other end of the phone. The Vixen jerked Elizabeth's gag back into place over her mouth.

'Oh dear,' said the Vixen into the phone, with mock sadness.

'Listen,' said Jack, angrily, 'if you harm her or Edward . . .'

'Oh, I'm sure there's no need for that,' said the Vixen sweetly. 'After all, you are going to give me the formula, aren't you.'

Jack looked at the others, who had all heard Elizabeth's scream down the phone. Whoever this woman was he couldn't afford to play games with her when Elizabeth and Edward's lives were at stake. He turned back to the phone.

'Yes, I will give you the formula,' he said.

'Good,' said the Vixen, pleased. 'I thought you might. Be at the Café de Kardomah in Lake Street at seven thirty this evening. Bring the formula and I'll let them both go, unharmed. And Mr Green . . . don't try any tricks.'

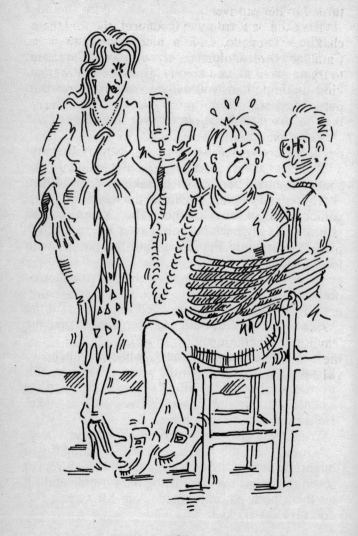

134

With that, the Vixen hung up the phone and then turned to her captives.

'The Café de Kardomah is so nice!' she told them chattily. 'They do such a nice Langouste à la Catalâne there. Unfortunately, you won't be there to try it. After all, you are my insurance against any kind of double-cross. But don't worry,' and she patted Edward gently on the cheek, 'I shall hurry back to you just as soon as I've got the formula.'

She moved across to a panel in the wall and opened it to reveal a wardrobe, from which she took a luxurious-looking matching coat and handbag. As she put the coat on she gave Elizabeth a long smile.

'There is, however, one little tiny white lie I told your dear brother Jack,' she said. 'The one about letting you go. Now that you've seen me and this place, I'm afraid it would be quite silly of me to do a foolish thing like that. So once I come back this evening, I'm afraid you're going to have to help me prepare a little meal: one of you for Cuddles, and one of you for my little fishes.'

And with that, she swept out of the apartment, leaving Elizabeth and Edward to stare in horror at the fishtank and the pool with Cuddles, the alligator, swimming around it hungrily.

CHAPTER SEVENTEEN

Negotiations

Mikhael Rinzikov sat slumped over his desk, crying noisily into his handkerchief.

'My poor Georgio!' he mourned. 'Turned into a fillet!'

Herman Shoemaker patted Rinzikov gently on the shoulder.

'There there, Mikhael,' he said in comforting tones. Poor guy, he thought, to lose an agent in the field like that.

He turned his attention to Butch Brooks, who was still standing stiffly to attention in front of the Russian's desk.

'Brooks,' he said sternly.

'Sir?' asked Butch.

'You are an idiot.'

Butch was offended.

'Pardon me, sir,' he said, 'but I was only doing my job.'

'Your job,' pointed out the CIA boss, 'was to get the formula back, not to leave your partner turning into jelly on the floor.' He patted the heaving shoulder of Mikhael Rinzikov again. 'We are partners on this case, Brooks, Russkies and Yankees working together to save the world.'

'Yes, sir,' said Butch.

'I didn't believe it would work at first,' continued Shoemaker, 'but I do now. Because we're all regular guys. We've all got courage, Brooks, whether we're Russian or American. We've all got guts! We've all got backbone . . . Except for your ex-partner, Georgio Nitzkov, who hasn't got any bones now at all!'

And this last point, Shoemaker shouted at Butch to drive the point home. Slumped on his desk, Rinzikov sobbed.

'Sir . . .' began Butch, determined to defend himself. He was interrupted by the phone on Rinzikov's desk ringing.

'Get that for me, please, my friend,' sniffled Rinzikov. 'I am too choked with emotion to talk.'

Shoemaker again patted the Russian sympathetically on the shoulder and picked up the phone.

'NFRSS High Command. CIA Officer Shoemaker speaking . . . What?!' He covered the mouthpiece and turned to the other two men. 'It's that Green guy!'

In Jack's flat Cynthia, Kate, Michael and Dorothy watched as Jack spoke to the CIA man, Cynthia keeping close to the tied-up Georgio.

'Listen very carefully,' said Jack. 'I have your agent, Georgio Nitzkov . . .'

There was a gasp from the other end of the line, and then Shoemaker asked, in a low voice so that he wouldn't upset his Russian colleague: 'Have you got him in a jar?'

Jack frowned, baffled by this question.

'In a jar?' he echoed. 'Of course not. He's alive and well and I am prepared to do a swap.'

In the NFRSS office, Shoemaker let out a whoop and thumped Rinzikov heartily.

'He says Georgio's alive and well!' he exclaimed.

'What?' said Rinzikov. Then he snatched the phone from Shoemaker, saying 'Let me talk to him! Let me talk to my poor Georgio!'

Jack motioned to Cynthia to bring Georgio over to the phone, which Cynthia did with the practised ease of an ex-Paratrooper.

'It's your boss,' Jack told him, and held the phone to Georgio's mouth.

'Comrade, I did not tell them anything,' said Georgio, urgently. 'Nothing. My lips are sealed. I am the man of iron.'

At that moment Cynthia tickled Georgio again, and Georgio dissolved into shrieks of laughter and collapsed on the floor. Mikhael Rinzikov held the phone away from his ear and turned to Shoemaker and Butch, an agonized expression on his face.

'They are torturing my poor Georgio!' he moaned.

'The heartless swines!' snarled Shoemaker.

But Rinzikov was once again listening to Jack talking on the phone.

'As I said, you can have him back unharmed, and the formula, if you help me get back my sister and her husband.'

Rinzikov frowned.

'What do you mean?' he asked. 'Where have they gone?'

'Someone has kidnapped them and has promised to exchange them in return for the formula,' said Jack.

Rinzikov put his hand over the phone and turned to Shoemaker, a look of indignation on his face.

'Have you kidnapped this Green man's sister and her husband?!' he demanded accusingly.

'Certainly not!' replied Shoemaker, with equal indignation.

Shoemaker, and also Butch, joined Rinzikov at the phone and all three now listened, to hear Jack saying impatiently: 'Hello? Hello?'

'Yes, Mr Green, I am here,' said Rinzikov.

'Good. Then here is the deal: If you help me deal with this woman who's kidnapped them, you get Georgio and the formula. Is it a deal?'

Rinzikov nodded vigorously.

'Yes. It is a deal. We will meet you tonight at a certain rendezvous that is very discreet . . .'

'Oh no you won't,' interrupted Jack firmly. '*I'll* tell you where we're going to meet . . .'

'Please, Mr Green,' urged Rinzikov beseechingly. 'We are the Secret Service, we know how to arrange these things best.'

'I don't care about that!' snorted Jack. 'The way you've arranged things so far . . .'

'Please,' implored Rinzikov again. 'The place I am going to suggest is ideal. Very discreet. The Café de Kardomah in Lake Street. We use it all the time. We'll meet at, say, seven thirty.'

Good Lord! thought Jack. The very place I was going to suggest!

'All right,' said Jack. 'We'll be there.'

And he hung up.

At the offices of the NFRSS, Rinzikov and Shoemaker were jubilant.

'Brilliant, Mikhael!' said Shoemaker. 'I couldn't have handled it better myself!'

'Yes! Tonight the formula will be ours!' exulted Rinzikov.

Butch frowned. There was still something he didn't understand.

'What about this woman who's kidnapped Green's family?' he asked. 'How did she get into the act?'

Shoemaker looked uncomfortable.

'I don't think we need to discuss it at this point . . .' he began.

Mikhael Rinzikov looked at Shoemaker, outraged.

'You mean you hired her as well?!' he demanded angrily. And then he put his hand to his mouth, realizing that he had made a *faux pas*. Shoemaker stared at Rinzikov.

'*As well*?' he echoed, outraged. 'You mean you also hired the Vixen? You double-crossing cheat!'

Then the two men stopped. What does it matter, thought Shoemaker. That was when we were opponents. Now we're on the same side. He put out his hand.

'No hard feelings, eh, Mikhael?'

Rinzikov took Shoemaker's hand and shook it firmly.

'None,' he said. 'From now on, we work together.'

Butch shook his head. He still wasn't exactly sure what was going on.

'Who is this "Vixen"?' he asked.

* * *

Back at Jack's flat they were all still recovering from the ordeal of Jack's phone conversation with the combined forces of the CIA and the NFRSS. Cynthia had taken charge yet again and was

141

currently in the kitchen brewing up a huge pot of tea.

'I really ought to phone my boss and let him know what's happening,' said Dorothy, a worried look on her face. 'After all, if the CIA and the NFRSS are going to be there . . .'

'I think she's right, Uncle Jack,' agreed Michael. 'After all, MI5 are supposed to be *our* Secret Service.'

Jack nodded.

'I don't see why not,' he said. 'The more the merrier.'

The sudden ringing of the phone made them all alert again. Everyone watched as Jack picked it up.

'4468. . . ?' he said.

The voice at the other end of the line was unmistakable.

'Listen carefully, Mr Green . . .' snarled Jose Cuervo. In the background Jack could hear the sounds of traffic. Cuervo was obviously making the call from a public call box somewhere. Jack put his hand over the mouthpiece and whispered to the others: 'It's that man again!'

In his ear he could hear Cuervo's voice: 'I have-a your friend Miss Taylor, the teacher, with me. I also have a gun. I want-a that formula and I want it tonight, or else I will kill her. Is that understood?'

Jack hesitated. What could he do? He'd already promised the formula to the mystery woman, and to the spy bosses. However, Miss Taylor's life was at stake. Somehow he had to buy time so that he could free her.

'All right,' he said, 'you can have it.'

At the other end of the line Cuervo gave a little cackle of delight.

'I am-a so happy to hear you say so, Mr Green,' he said. 'Bring it to me at . . .'

Jack cut him short.

'No you don't,' said Jack, '*I'll* make the arrangements . . .'

'You forget, Mr Green,' said Cuervo menacingly. '*I* am the one who holds-a the hostage. *I* say where. We will meet at the Café de Kardomah in Lake Street at seven thirty. Be there, or else.'

Then there was just the dull tone of the phone as Cuervo hung up. Jack replaced the phone and turned to look at the others, astonished. The Café de Kardomah again! Well well well! It must be a regular haunt for spies and villains!

'Don't think I'm interfering Jack,' ventured Cynthia after a pause, 'but I think you're being a bit ambitious with all this.'

'She's right, Uncle Jack,' said Michael. 'You can't meet *all* these people tonight.'

'Yes I can,' said Jack, still a bit bemused by it all. 'They all suggested we meet in the same place *and* at the same time.'

'What?!'

'Yes,' said Jack. 'According to Georgio's boss it's a very discreet secret rendezvous: the Café de Kardomah.'

Kate and Michael looked at each other, and then burst out laughing. Jack, Cynthia and Dorothy looked at them, puzzled.

'What's so funny?' asked Dorothy.

'It's not that discreet!' chuckled Michael.

'What do you mean?' said Jack.

Kate and Michael laughed again.

'We've been invited to a birthday party there

tonight by Peregrine Picklethwaite, the richest kid in our school!' chuckled Kate.

'Not that we were going,' said Michael. 'Peregrine Picklethwaite is only in the First Year and, knowing his parents, it'll be a real baby's party. Yuk!'

'Right,' agreed Kate. 'With party hats and babies' games. Not a *real* party. I bet his mum even has a clown or something silly coming.'

'I don't care,' said Jack. 'You're going. Think of it as protection.'

CHAPTER EIGHTEEN

The Café de Kardomah

The manager of the Café de Kardomah, Eduardo de Blanc (previously known as Ted White), was fed up. For some years his restaurant had been used by spies of many nations as a meeting place to exchange plans and secrets, but usually only one such meeting at a time, which didn't interfere with the normal running of his restaurant. Then today he had received a clutch of phone calls: the first from Herman Shoemaker of the CIA, informing him that the CIA *and* the NFRSS would be arranging an exchange there tonight; the second from that weird and very dangerous South American, Jose Cuervo, telling him that *he* would be at the Café de Kardomah that night for an exchange; and the third from the 'Vixen' – (at the very thought of her, Eduardo shuddered; now there was someone who was *really* dangerous) – telling him that *she* was arranging an exchange that night at the Café de Kardomah.

On top of all that, Shoemaker had informed him that he would need to place one of his agents in the Café, working undercover as a waiter. (Eduardo had hoped and prayed that it wouldn't be their agent Butch Brooks. Not only was the man a numbskull in his opinion, he was also notoriously clumsy and Eduardo didn't fancy having Butch Brooks carrying plates of soup around in his beautiful restaurant. And when the CIA agent had arrived early that evening to be kitted out as a waiter, it had, of course, been Butch Brooks.

On top of all that, groaned Eduardo, there was this children's birthday party now in full swing at tables three and four!

Not that Eduardo had anything against children. Provided they weren't in his restaurant he could take them or leave them but, from his experience, children's birthday parties meant mess: sooner or later a child would spill something on the table or on the floor, or another would be sick from eating too much.

The door of the restaurant was pushed open and Eduardo leapt smartly to attention, switching on his professional smile at once. Then his smile eased off a little. It was Shoemaker, the CIA boss, one of the men who was causing him the headaches that he knew he was going to suffer this evening.

'Good evening, sir,' he said politely, keeping up the pretence of Never Having Seen This Man Before.

'Good evening,' said Shoemaker. 'Table for one, please.'

Eduardo showed Shoemaker to a table. Immediately Butch appeared from the kitchens, (coming out of the 'Out' door, Eduardo was relieved to notice) and went to Shoemaker, ostensibly to take his order but in reality to fill his boss in on what had happened in the restaurant so far. (What had happened was very little, actually, except for the children at the birthday tables singing 'Happy Birthday' to Peregrine Picklethwaite three times so far.)

Eduardo saw the door of the restaurant open, and

immediately hurried to open it wider. This time it was Mikhael Rinzikov, the boss of the NFRSS. Eduardo gave him the same smile he had given Shoemaker.

'Good evening, sir,' he smiled. He indicated towards Shoemaker, who was having his order taken by Butch. 'Would you like to share with the other gentleman?'

This seemed logical to Eduardo. After all, the CIA and the NFRSS were now working together. It would also save him a table. Rinzikov shook his head. He and Shoemaker had decided that it would be unwise to let the Vixen know they were working as one on this project.

'A table for one,' he said.

Eduardo forced a smile.

'Certainly, sir,' he said, and escorted Rinzikov to the table next to Shoemaker's.

Butch, meanwhile, was at the birthday tables taking orders from the children, most of which were for more cakes and ice cream, and at the same time keeping a close watch on everything that was happening in the restaurant. He had his orders: to get Georgio back, and to get the formula. Well, as sure as his name was Butch Brooks, that was exactly what he was going to do. A movement at the door caught his eye and he turned in time to see the door of the restaurant open and the manager hurry forward to welcome the newly arrived customer. Was it the Green guy? Butch sucked in his breath. Jumping Jehosaphat! It was M himself, the Head of MI5! That Dorothy Greckle woman must have tipped him off about the meeting.

Eduardo took M's coat. Not another spy! he groaned. Aloud he said: 'Good evening, sir.'

'Good evening,' said M. 'A table for one.'

Another table for one! groaned Eduardo again. At this rate he wouldn't have any spare tables left for his real customers.

M sat down and looked around him. He recognized Shoemaker and Rinzikov, who, of course, also recognized him, but none of the three men gave any sign of knowing each other. As Butch was busy with bringing the cakes and ice creams for the children at the birthday tables, Eduardo's regular waiter, Hans, took out his order pad and went to Rinzikov and M to take their orders.

M was half-way through giving his order to Hans when he stopped as the door of the restaurant opened and a Latin-looking man came in. The man had one arm draped around a woman, and the other, covered in scarf, pressed into her side. M was sure that beneath the scarf the man was pointing a gun.

In this M was right. Cuervo had Miss Taylor well and truly covered. He was taking no chances; she had already kicked him once and his leg still hurt. Eduardo approached Cuervo with his fixed restaurant manager's smile.

'Good evening, sir, madam,' he said. 'For two?'

Cuervo regarded Eduardo suspiciously.

'For two what?' he demanded.

Inwardly, Eduardo sighed. He hadn't realized he was dealing with quite such an idiot.

'The table,' he explained.

Cuervo shook his head.

'No, just one table will be enough,' he said.

Then, without waiting for Eduardo to escort them, he shepherded Miss Taylor towards an empty table near to the two doors marked 'IN' and 'OUT' which led to the kitchen. If there was trouble, he wanted an escape route.

Miss Taylor was silent, but fuming. This odious man! As if it wasn't enough that he kept pressing this gun into her side, he would also insist on yammering on to her about his 'Glorious Revolution'. Well when all this was over she would give him a piece of her mind! The man was certainly no gentleman!

The door of the restaurant opened again, and now everyone took notice as in walked Jack and Cynthia (with their arms firmly around the shoulders of Georgio Nitzkov) and behind them Dorothy, Kate and Michael.

Eduardo hurried to greet them, praying fervently that they wouldn't each ask for a table for one – that would be another six tables used up.

'Good evening,' he smiled. 'Are you all together?'

Jack shook his head and smiled.

'No,' he said, and he indicated towards Cynthia and Georgio. 'We three are.'

Eduardo suddenly realized that the reason for the close comradeship between these three was because the man in the middle had his hands tied behind his back. *This* must be the exchange that everyone was waiting for.

At that moment the kid whose birthday party it was, Peregrine Picklethwaite, turned and caught sight of Kate and Michael.

'Hey, Michael! Kate!' he called delightedly. 'You made it!'

Kate and Michael looked at their uncle, who nodded, and Kate and Michael went across the restaurant to join the other children at the birthday table.

'Go with them,' Jack whispered to Dorothy, 'just in case anything happens.'

Dorothy nodded and followed Kate and Michael, and the three of them crammed into the celebratory crowd. As she passed M, Dorothy gave him the briefest of glances. She didn't acknowledge him. After all, she reasoned, she didn't want to let the CIA and the NFRSS know that they knew each other.

M, for his part, was put out. Rude woman, he thought, ignoring me like that!

Jack indicated an empty table at the very centre of the restaurant.

'That one will do fine for us,' he said. Then he and Cynthia guided Georgio to it and sat down.

'How am I going to eat with my hands tied behind my back?' complained Georgio.

'I'll ask for a straw,' said Jack coolly.

He looked around the restaurant. He nodded to Miss Taylor, who was sitting crushed against the mysterious man who had started off this whole caper. Miss Taylor nodded back. The man scowled.

Jack looked around the rest of the restaurant. The three men sitting on their own at three separate tables must be M, the CIA boss and the NFRSS boss, he thought. But there was no sign of a woman who might be the Vixen. He looked up as a shadow fell across the table, and found himself looking at the other man who he had believed had been a plain-clothes policeman along with Georgio Nitzkov. Butch nodded to Georgio.

'Don't worry, Georgio,' he whispered, 'we'll get you out of this. We've got this place surrounded.'

'If you try anything,' warned Jack quietly, 'I'll eat the formula.'

This made Butch stop in his tracks. Eat the formula?! Jumping Jeremiah! Butch gave Jack a hard stare that should have made Jack shiver in his shoes, but didn't, and went back into the kitchen.

Another shadow fell across the table. Was this the Vixen? wondered Jack, looking up again. It wasn't, it was someone dressed as a clown. Jack examined the clown closely. Perhaps it was the Vixen in disguise, or perhaps it was a messenger from her?

'Are you the party for the entertainment?' asked the clown.

'What sort of entertainment?' asked Jack guardedly, wondering if this was coded language.

'The birthday entertainment,' said the clown. 'Are you Peregrine Picklethwaite?'

Jack grinned.

'I think you're needed over there,' he said, and he pointed towards the children at the birthday table.

The clown looked across at the children, singing and making faces at each other and stuffing their faces with cakes and ice cream, and a shudder went through him. He had begged and hoped and prayed that it wouldn't be children again. He didn't like children. Or, more to the point, children didn't like him, and to be a clown that children didn't like was asking for trouble. The trouble was that the clown saw himself as a sophisticated actor who should have been doing Shakespeare plays. He wanted to be appreciated for his subtle wit and pearls of wisdom. Children didn't see it that way. They wanted a clown who slipped on banana skins and hurt his bottom; who got custard pies in the face; who could juggle and do magic tricks. This clown couldn't juggle and he couldn't do magic tricks, and he couldn't tell jokes either. Sometimes he thought he was in the wrong job, but he reflected that it was better than being a postman, which was what he had been before. At least being a clown meant that he didn't get bitten by dogs. Now he got bitten by children instead.

'Hello children!' he cried as he forced his huge greasepainted lips into a wide grin and squeaked his squeaky nose.

'Aarghh!!' screamed a little girl, terrified at this apparition. Another child threw an ice cream which hit the clown on his squeaky nose. The clown smiled hopefully. Would that raise a laugh? Maybe it would have but another child had just been sick, which the other children found much more interesting. The clown sighed and pulled three bananas out of his pocket.

'I will now juggle these bananas,' he announced, and began to throw them into the air.

Eduardo was intent on keeping an eye on things, and praying silently that the clown would keep the children occupied, when the door of the restaurant opened and in glided the Vixen. Eduardo leaped to attention immediately, and then swept low in a fawning bow.

'Good evening, mademoiselle,' he said in a syrupy voice. 'May I say how enchanting you look this evening.'

'You may,' purred the Vixen. She looked around the restaurant and her gaze lit on Jack, Cynthia and Georgio at the centre of the restaurant. She pointed to the empty table next to them. 'I'll have that table, Eduardo.'

'Certainly, mademoiselle,' said Eduardo. He

picked up a menu. 'If mademoiselle will follow me.'

He led her to the table she had indicated, and all eyes followed her. There was no mistaking that the Vixen had a stunning presence. Miss Taylor particularly noticed something about her.

'That woman has got the very same handbag that I have!' she said indignantly.

'Shuttup!' growled Cuervo, and pressed the gun a little harder into Miss Taylor's ribs.

'May I take your order?' Eduardo asked the Vixen, his pen poised above his pad.

The Vixen studied the menu.

'Yes,' she said. 'I'll have a still mineral water . . . and the Boeuf Incroyable.' And she returned the menu to Eduardo with a sweet smile. 'Make the meat very rare. You know how I like it, Eduardo. Still bleeding.'

Eduardo shuddered as he took the menu, but forced a smile and hoped that the Vixen didn't notice his shiver of fear. The Vixen had noticed, and she smiled as she watched Eduardo disappear towards the kitchen.

At Jack and Cynthia's table, Georgio was feeling fed up.

'Why doesn't anyone take our order?' he complained. 'I'm hungry.'

'Shut up,' said Jack. 'Business first.'

The Vixen smiled across at Jack.

'Good evening, Mr Green,' she smiled. 'We meet at last.' She nodded towards Georgio and Cynthia. 'I see you have company.'

'Call it insurance,' said Jack politely.

The Vixen smiled at Georgio and Cynthia.

'Good evening, Mr and Mrs Insurance.'

Butch had been watching this exchange between Jack and the Vixen, waiting for one of them to do something so that he could make his move. So intently was he watching them that, as he headed back towards the kitchen, his eyes still on Jack, he didn't notice that he was heading towards the wrong door. He reached the 'OUT' door and pushed. There was a crash and a yell of annoyance from the other side. Then the door swung open to reveal Hans the waiter surrounded by broken plates and covered in soup.

'Idiot!' snarled Hans.

'Gee, I'm sorry . . .' began Butch, but Eduardo was already on the scene, ordering Hans to go and get cleaned up and telling Butch to be more careful. Jack was too concerned with the business in hand to take too much notice of all this.

'Where are Elizabeth and Edward?' Jack asked the Vixen. 'You said you would be bringing them with you.'

'They are outside, locked in the car. I thought it unwise to bring them into such a public place as this. Do you have the formula?'

'Of course,' said Jack, 'and you can have it after I have seen Edward and Elizabeth.'

The Vixen gave a mocking, 'sad' smile.

'Mr Green,' she pouted. 'Don't you trust me?'

Jack shook his head.

'No further than I'd trust a tarantula. Let me see Elizabeth and Edward.'

'Certainly,' cooed the Vixen. 'First, let me have the formula.'

'Not before I have seen my sister and her husband,' said Jack doggedly.

The Vixen smiled. Beneath the smile she was beginning to lose her temper with this man.

'Do you know what I think, Mr Green?' she said. 'I don't think you have the formula at all.'

'I would hardly insult your intelligence by coming here without it,' said Jack.

'Prove it,' said the Vixen.

Jack thought it over. At this exact moment there was very little else he could do if he was to get Elizabeth and Edward back.

'Keep your eye on Georgio,' Jack whispered to Cynthia. Then he reached into his inside pocket and pulled out a sheet of paper, and held it up so that the Vixen could see it.

'Here,' he said.

This was what Herman Shoemaker had been waiting for.

'Go, Butch!' he yelled.

Jack hastily snatched back the formula as Butch threw aside the plates of food he was carrying and leapt at Jack. Suddenly Jose Cuervo realized what was going on. That waiter was trying to get hold of the formula! *His* formula!

'Oh no you don't!' he yelled. 'That's-a mine!'

And Cuervo leapt out of his chair, grabbed hold of Butch and threw him bodily to one side. Butch stumbled and crashed into Peregrine Picklethwaite at the birthday table, sending Peregrine's head tumbling forward, face-first, into a plate of jelly and cream.

'Yurkkk!' yelled Peregrine.

Peregrine stood up, looking around for the culprit who had done this, and his eyes lighted on Butch. No one does that to me on my birthday and gets away with it! thought Peregrine, and he picked up a handful of ice cream and hurled it at Butch, who was just getting up to launch an attack on Jose Cuervo.

Shoemaker saw this and leapt to the defence of his agent.

'Look out behind you, Butch!' he yelled.

Butch looked, saw what was coming, and leapt to one side. The ice cream just missed Butch, and scored a direct hit on Herman Shoemaker's shirt front.

Shoemaker looked down in astonishment at the ice cream sliding down inside his shirt. No one treats the boss of the CIA that way! he fumed, and he picked up his melon starter and threw it back at Peregrine. It was the worst thing he could have done. The next minute Shoemaker was under attack from a hail of food from the birthday table as all the other children joined in, in defence of their friend.

Cuervo, meanwhile, was engaged in a tussle with Cynthia, and not doing very well. Caramba! thought Cuervo as Cynthia put him in an armlock and forced him to the floor. This woman would be a wonderful asset to my Revolutionary Army!

The Vixen, seeing all this food flying across the restaurant, had taken refuge by the kitchen, determined that she wasn't going to have her new outfit from Emmanuel ruined by food.

Miss Taylor now realized that she was free of Cuervo and his menacing gun and headed for the door, intent on summoning the Police. She never got there. A flying cream puff, intended for Shoemaker, scored a direct hit on the side of her head.

'Who did that?' she yelled, enraged. And she picked up a bowl of soup from a nearby table and

159

hurled it at her assailant. It was at this moment that Hans the waiter returned, having just put on a clean jacket. The bowl of soup that Miss Taylor threw hit him fair and square on the chest, soaking him once more with soup. This was too much for Hans. With a roar of rage he picked up the nearest thing to hand, which happened to be a banana split, and threw it at Miss Taylor, hitting her on the face with it.

The clown had long ago given up trying to entertain the children. His bananas had vanished within the first few seconds of the food fight for ammunition and all he could do was cower on the floor and wish that he was back on his postal round. Even being chased by dogs was better than this.

Jack sat in the middle of all the chaos, bewildered. Suddenly he saw a hand reaching for the formula. He was about to snatch it back, when Georgio did the job for him, kicking out with his feet in a determined effort to make sure that no one but the NFRSS got their hands on the formula! Mikhael Rinzikov, the boss of the NFRSS, clutched his leg and staggered backwards.

'You idiot!' he howled at Georgio. 'It's me!'

And with that, he fell over. Cuervo had by now broken free of Cynthia, and when he saw Rinzikov on the floor he assumed, wrongly, that the NFRSS boss had somehow managed to get hold of the formula.

'It's-a mine!' he yelled, and leapt upon Rinzikov.

'Oh no it isn't!' cried out M, and he dived in, determined to get the formula back for MI5. If that Greckle woman wasn't going to do anything about it, then *he* would! Within a few seconds nearly everyone else was in the huge scrum on the floor of the restaurant.

Dorothy, Kate and Michael had managed to stay clear of the food fight and now crept over to join Uncle Jack.

'Where are Mum and Dad?' asked Kate.

'Where's that flashy woman?' asked Michael.

Jack looked around, and then realized with a shock that, amid all the chaos, the Vixen had managed to get away.

'She's gone!' he said, horrified.

Kate let out a cry.

'And she's going to kill Mum and Dad!' she wailed.

CHAPTER NINETEEN

The Last Battle

A sudden scream from Miss Taylor made them look round, assuming that she had been struck by a particularly messy piece of food. Miss Taylor, however, was glaring in annoyance into her handbag. Or, rather, what she thought was her handbag. She had opened it to take out a tissue to wipe some of the food off her face, and discovered that – although it had looked like her handbag – it wasn't.

'That woman's taken my handbag!' she yelled furiously.

'What?' said Jack.

'She had the same handbag as me,' said Miss Taylor. 'She must have picked it up by mistake, and now she's gone off with it.'

Jack snatched the bag from Miss Taylor and emptied the contents on a table, searching for a clue as to where the Vixen's hideout was located. He was sure that that was where the Vixen was keeping Elizabeth and Edward prisoner, and unless he found them very soon . . .

Yes! Jack picked up the Vixen's driving licence, and there on it was her address: The Apartment, Dobson's Old Warehouse, 22 Bracket Street. Jack grabbed Kate and Michael's hands.

'Let's go, kids!' he yelled excitedly. 'You too, Dorothy! I think I know where she's holding Elizabeth and Edward! Let's just hope I'm right.'

The Vixen was furious! All that effort and for nothing! She had even seen the formula, been close enough to touch it, and had lost it! And to make matters worse she had picked up the wrong handbag at the Café de Kardomah!

As she went upwards in the lift towards the top floor of the warehouse and her luxury apartment, she considered the situation. Her cover was blown, of that there was no doubt. Once they looked inside her handbag and found her driver's licence with her address on it, they would be here. It was lucky that the door of the warehouse in the street had an electronic lock that only opened to the sound of her voice. That way no one would be able to follow her in, even when they discovered her address.

She would have to flee the country, that was the only answer. Luckily, she kept a car in the basement of the warehouse for just such an eventuality as this. Inside the glove compartment were all the documents she would need for a quick getaway: a forged passport, a fake driver's licence, and credit cards in a variety of names. The basement of the warehouse was connected by a tunnel to a building some two blocks away, so even if they surrounded her building they would never catch her. She would simply descend in the secret lift to the basement, into the car and away. But first she had some tidying up to do.

The lift stopped and the Vixen stepped out and into her apartment. It was much the same as she had left it. Cuddles her alligator – she would miss him, poor sweet thing, but she was sure the RSPCA would find him a good home – reclined at the bottom of the pool in the floor. Elizabeth and Edward were still tied together, back-to-back on their chairs as she had left them, but they had managed to slip the gags down from their mouths.

Elizabeth and Edward watched the Vixen warily as she came in. It was obvious from her manner that things had not gone well. The Vixen angrily threw Miss Taylor's handbag into the pool. Cuddles was stirred into action by this and pounced upon the handbag, his tail threshing the water as he did so. Cuddles took one mouthful of the bag and realized it wasn't proper food. He spat it out of the pool back on to the floor, where it landed with a wet thud.

The Vixen stood, hands on hips and looked at Elizabeth and Edward, breathing in deeply and trying to regain her composure.

'I have never been so humiliated in my life!' she said.

Elizabeth and Edward didn't like to ask her what had gone wrong. Elizabeth assumed it was something to do with Jack; her brother was always doing things that led to other people getting into trouble.

The Vixen paced around them, clawing the nails of one hand into the palm of the other. Yes, she would have her revenge on Mr Jack Green. When he finally arrived, he would find his sister and brother-in-law all right. Or, rather, bits of them. The thought brought a smile back to her face, and Elizabeth and Edward grew even more nervous, because the smile was so nasty, so malicious that even Elizabeth decided it was better to remain silent. The Vixen leaned towards them.

'I must tell you that I'm very, very, very angry,' she told them, though by now her voice had calmed down a bit as she tried to halt her temper. 'Would you like to know what I do when I get angry? I calm myself down by making a chopping list.'

Elizabeth frowned, puzzled.

'Don't you mean "shopping" list?' she queried.

The Vixen shook her head.

'I know what I mean,' she said.

With that, the Vixen went to a cupboard hidden in one of her walls and opened it, and took out a large axe with a shiny and very sharp blade.

* * *

Jack, Kate, Michael and Dorothy, meanwhile, had pulled up in Jack's car outside Dobson's Old Warehouse in Bracket Street. Jack immediately ran to the metal door but found that there was no way to open it. In place of a lock it had a small grille set in the door, but no amount of tugging or poking at it made any impression on the door at all. Jack was looking around desperately for a way to get into the warehouse, when he saw the disused warehouse next to Dobson's, separated from it by a narrow alley. He ran back to the car.

'I'm going in there,' he told Dorothy and the children. 'I might be able to find a way across to where she's holding them. While I'm doing that, call the Police and tell them what's happened and where we are. They might be able to find a way in.'

With that, Jack ran to the disused warehouse at the other side of the alley.

Luckily for Jack, the door into the warehouse was broken and he was able to squeeze through. Inside, the warehouse smelt old and fusty and there were cobwebs hanging from holes in the ceiling. The warehouse obviously hadn't been used for some years. If he could get to a higher floor, thought Jack, he might be able to find a way across the alley into Dobson's warehouse.

In the gloom Jack just managed to make out a flight of stairs. He went across to them, tripping over debris as he did so, and started to go up. An ominous creaking underfoot warned him to beware, the wooden stairs were rotting and in some places had already broken. If he trod on a rotten piece he would go through and crash back down to the floor. Keeping close to the edge, he carried on climbing.

Jack discovered that every time he came to a landing he could see through the empty rooms of the disused warehouse, across the alley towards Dobson's warehouse. At each landing he stopped, but each time there was nothing across the alley except blackness.

It was on the fifth landing that he saw the light across the alley. That was where they must be!

He began to hurry across the landing into the large empty room, when he heard a creaking underfoot. Suddenly, part of the floor gave way. Jack just managed to step back in time to save himself from crashing down along with the floor, to the ground five floors below.

He let out a long sigh of relief, then he skirted the edges of what remained of the floor and crept gingerly across the empty room to the window. At the window he found that the glass had long since gone and there was a balcony outside. Carefully, testing the concrete first, he climbed out through the broken window and out on to the balcony.

Yes, he could see them, through a large window directly across the alley from this warehouse:

Elizabeth and Edward tied back-to-back in a luxury apartment, and the woman who called herself the Vixen pacing slowly up and down, holding something in her hands. What was it? Jack craned forward to see, and then let out a gasp of horror. She was holding an axe, and there was no doubt what she intended to do with it! He had to find a way to stop her, but how?

He looked around the balcony for something he could use: a stone, a brick, something he could throw through the window and, with any luck, hit her. A coil of rope caught his eye and he picked it up. He tugged it between his hands to test it. It seemed to be strong enough. If he could tie a loop in one end and throw it over the hook that projected from the roof of Dobson's warehouse, just one floor above him across the alley, he could swing across . . .

Jack shook his head. The idea was insane! The sort of thing that only happened in *Tarzan* or pirate films. In real life it would never work. So many things could go wrong: for a start he doubted if he could lassoo the loop of rope over the hook. For another, how could he judge the length of the rope? Say it stretched? If that happened he would thud into the wall *below* the window. On the other hand, if the rope was too short he would hit Dobson's warehouse *above* the window. Either way he would knock himself out and fall to the cobbles of the alley below.

As Jack watched, the Vixen raised the axe and approached Elizabeth and Edward, an evil smile on her face. She was saying something, and whatever she was saying was making Elizabeth and Edward shrink back from her in fear.

Jack looked down at the rope in his hands. He was

left with very little choice. Even if he failed to get through the window of her apartment, the commotion he would make in failing might make the Vixen think twice, and at least he might save Elizabeth and Edward. Carefully, Jack began to tie the end of the rope into a large loop.

* * *

The Vixen ran her finger along the edge of the blade. Beautifully sharp! Just one stroke would be all it would take to chop off a head! She gave Elizabeth a slow smile.

'I feel a bit better now, you'll be glad to know,' she said. 'But then, doing good always makes me feel better.'

Elizabeth gulped. Better to try to keep this mad woman talking, she thought. Sooner or later *someone* must arrive to rescue them.

'Doing good?' asked Elizabeth.

The Vixen nodded.

'Yes,' she said. 'Feeding my dear little pets. They're always so happy after a meal.'

And she brought the axe to within striking distance of Elizabeth.

* * *

Across the alley Jack judged the distance from the balcony to the hook that was jutting out from the roof of the warehouse opposite. Well, he thought, this is it. Now or never. He took aim, held the loop of the rope the way he'd seen cowboys do in films when they lassooed cattle, and threw it. The rope sailed up towards the hook, hovered in the air, and then plunged back down towards the alley. Missed! cursed Jack.

* * *

Edward gulped. He could feel the sweat running down his face. This wasn't at all funny. That man ruining his matchstick model of Big Ben had been bad enough, but this. . . !!

'Excuse me?' he said, his voice quavering slightly.

The Vixen looked at Edward questioningly.

'Yes?' she said.

'Can . . . can we have a last request?' asked Edward.

The Vixen smiled.

'Certainly,' she purred. 'What is it?'

'Can we go home?' asked Edward.

By way of answer the Vixen gave a low throaty laugh and wielded the axe over her shoulder, ready to strike.

'I do *so* like a man with a sense of humour,' she said.

* * *

Across the alley, on the balcony, Jack held the rope loosely in his right hand, taking deep breaths and telling himself to calm down, calm down . . .

He took aim again at the hook on the roof of the building opposite, swung the rope back . . . then threw it. Again the loop sailed towards the hook, hovered in the air, and then dropped over it! Done it! thought Jack exultantly. He pulled on the rope, tightening the loop. All he had to hope now was that the hook was firmly fixed to the brickwork of Dobson's warehouse. If it wasn't he would crash right down to the hard ground below. He gave the rope a tug. It seemed to hold. He took a firm handhold on the rope at what he hoped was the right distance to get him in through the Vixen's window. He pulled on the rope again, to test it, then he took a deep breath . . . and jumped, launching himself into space across the alley . . .

* * *

The Vixen, raising the axe above her head, gave Edward a last smile.

'Goodbye . . .' she said sweetly.

There was a crash of shattering glass and the Vixen whirled round just in time to see Jack come hurtling through her apartment window on the end of a length of rope. Jack let go of the rope and rolled across the floor, stopping with a thud against the far wall. The Vixen hissed through her teeth. That damned interfering Jack Green again! She moved towards Jack and raised the axe above her head.

'Look out!' yelled Elizabeth.

As the Vixen brought the axe down, Jack rolled to one side just in time, and the blade of the axe crashed down on to the floor, embedding itself through the carpet and into the wood beneath. The Vixen tugged at the handle of the axe, trying to free it. Jack stumbled to his feet and smiled at her.

'Game to me, I think,' he said.

The Vixen snarled.

'That's what you think!' she snapped.

Without warning the Vixen belted Jack with a hard punch on his nose. Jack staggered back, stunned, and as he did so his foot caught the edge of the pool. The next second he had toppled over and

fallen in, straight on top of Cuddles the alligator!

Elizabeth and Edward screamed in unison when they saw what had happened. There was a flurry in the water, and then Jack leapt out, just managing to get clear as the alligator's jaws snapped shut behind him.

Edward turned to see what the Vixen was up to, and saw her just about to slip into what looked like a cupboard set in one wall.

'Look!' he called.

Jack and Elizabeth looked, and the door in the wall slid shut. The next thing they heard was the sound of machinery.

'It's a lift!' said Elizabeth. 'She's getting away!'

'We'll let the police catch her,' said Jack. 'The main thing now is to get you two out of this.'

And Jack set to work untying their ropes. As soon as Elizabeth and Edward were free once more Elizabeth began to look for the button inside the apartment that would open the street door and let in Dorothy, Kate, Michael and the Police.

For his part, Jack picked up Miss Taylor's chewed handbag from the floor and tossed it in his hands.

'The clue that brought me here,' he said. 'I suppose we'd better get it back to Miss Taylor.'

* * *

At the Café de Kardomah the police were being kept busy. It had taken them some time to bring the food fight under control, and now they were busy scraping off food from everyone so that they could identify them and place them under arrest. They were just in the process of arresting the clown, when the door of the restaurant opened and Jack entered, with

173

Elizabeth, Edward, Kate, Michael and Dorothy following behind him. Under one arm Jack had Miss Taylor's handbag, and he gave it back to her now. The police, wondering who this new batch of people were, stopped what they were doing.

'Are you responsible for this?' the sergeant in charge demanded of Jack.

Jack debated to himself how he should answer. In a way, he supposed he was.

'Can we discuss that later?' he asked. 'Right now, I have a very important statement to make to everyone.'

At once all eyes in the restaurant fell on Jack.

'This whole business has occurred because everyone's been chasing after a formula. Well, to put an end to it, and to stop this from going on any further in this ridiculous fashion, here it is. A copy for everyone.'

And with that Jack pulled a bunch of papers, each with the same chemical formula on them, from his inside pocket. Then he, Kate and Michael began handing them out to everyone in the restaurant.

M, the CIA and NFRSS bosses, and Jose Cuervo looked at each other, and then at Jack, in shocked outrage. What on earth was the fellow playing at?! Didn't he realize that this was the formula for the most dangerous gas ever known! Yet here he was handing it out to all and sundry as if it was confetti!

'There,' said Jack when he had finished distributing them. 'Now you've all got a copy, there should be no arguments.'

It was Herman Shoemaker who first suspected what was going on.

'What's the catch?' he demanded.

Jack smiled.

'I wondered when you'd realize,' he said. 'Tell them, Cynthia.'

Cynthia Birdwood removed some ice cream from her face and beamed at the assembled gathering.

'Frankly,' she said, 'one look at this formula convinced me that it was bad news. So, Jack and I discussed what to do about it; and because we felt that the formula was far too dangerous as it stood, I've made a small adjustment to it.'

'What sort of adjustment?' asked M.

'I've omitted the molecules that trigger the gas that poisons the particles that penetrate the phosphates that pollute the perimeter,' replied Cynthia.

Everyone looked blankly at her, none the wiser. Mikhael Rinzikov was the first to speak.

'What does that do?' he asked.

'It turns it into a harmless puff of air,' said Cynthia with a proud smile.

Shoemaker threw away the formula he'd just been given in disgust. This was the last thing anyone needed, *harmless* weapons!

'Where's the piece of paper with the original formula on it?' he demanded.

'That?' said Jack airily. 'Oh, we burnt it. The formula for the death gas doesn't exist any more.'

The three spy bosses and Jose Cuervo looked at one another, helpless. All that chasing around . . . for this! Nothing!

It was M, shaking his head sorrowfully, who approached Jack. The man was a pain in the neck, he had to admit, but on this one he'd outwitted them all! One had to admire the man.

'Tell me, Mr Green,' he said, forcing what he

hoped looked like an inviting smile. 'Have you ever thought of working for Intelligence?'

Jack grinned and put his arms around Kate and Michael.

'We already *do* work for intelligence,' he said. 'We're saving the planet. Right, Kate and Michael?'

'Right, Uncle Jack!' said Kate and Michael, grinning.